- My 1
KAREN & CATRINN

NA

Buffett (signature)

THE DEADLY PRIEST

Looking back at his achievements,

Jerome Helms

could not help

but have a

happy sense of

well-being,

except for one glitch

which had taken place

ten years ago.

The Deadly Priest

Jerome has been a priest for the past 12 years, having graduated with honors, an "A" student and Valedictorian. It was not his desire to join the priesthood, following in his father's footsteps. His decision was prompted when his Dad decided to rejoin the priesthood after the sudden passing of Jerome's mother, Esther. She died from a massive heart attack, mainly due to stress brought about by his father's infidelity.

Father Jerome's mother had been in and out of hospitals, seeing almost every heart specialist in and around their small town of Lowell, Boston and even neighboring New England, for the better part of ten years, prior to her passing.

Jerome's unswerving conclusion was that his father was the main contributing factor to his mother's death. He felt sure that his old man had only returned to the priesthood to make amends for the wrong things he had done to his wife while she was alive. Father Jerome was convinced that, had his father been a better person to his Mom, she might still be alive. In his humble opinion, she died more of stress from his father, than from her heart condition.

Jerome and his twin brother Ray was the eldest of six siblings, none of whom would stay beside the aging priest. Except for Father Jerome. He stayed with his father the longest, most likely because of his religious convictions.

It was never Jerome's desire to become a priest. It was his Father's insistent persuasion. Fr. Thom, as they referred to him, short for Thomas, now himself 73 years and ailing, insisted that Jerome follow in his footsteps. To keep the peace, Jerome obliged.

CHAPTER ONE

Twenty years ago, most children did not have the option of choosing their own careers. It was normal for parents to influence their kids on a career choice. Fr. Thom was no different. Therefore, it meant if the parent was a lawyer then it was expected that the son or daughter would follow in that field. Jerome's father was a priest so Jerome had no choice. His first choice was to become a lawyer or a medical doctor. He reluctantly entered college to become a priest but he was influenced by his twin brother Ray and Ray's taste for bar hopping, girlfriends, pimps and prostitutes. Ray was living a colorful lifestyle in New York City and Fr. Jerome found some pleasure being in such company. He even experimented with cocaine and at times, marijuana, just to be cool in the presence of his brother and friends. After all, everyone around him was doing it, how different could he be?

Whenever Fr. Jerome was in New York, "Ray's town", Ray would take him to those wild parties, and being weak, Fr. Jerome made it a point to be in the Big Apple whenever he had time. Jerome always spent his vacation time with his brother.

Ray introduced him to quite a few beautiful women, some of whom were strung out on drugs. Those were the ones Jerome especially liked because those were usually an easy score, pretty much like prostitutes, just that they did not hang out on the street corners. Ray even introduced him to a pair of lesbians who performed a live sex act in a nearby strip joint.

Fr. Jerome found it difficult to believe two extremely pretty women, did not have men in their lives. He had his doubts until he saw the act a second time at a private party, up close and personal. To him, a lifetime without sex would be like a death sentence.

Jerome knew that he had made a life-altering decision to become a Catholic Priest. Now that he had satisfied his father's wishes, what about his own wishes?, he thought in passing. He often had regrets, but somehow his thoughts were compounded whenever he was in Ray's company.

Initially, his first plan was to do as his father did. Finish the priesthood, leave, get married and have a family. Then return to the priesthood after completing the fun side of life. It was now Jerome's twelfth year in the priesthood and he had just returned from his vacation time with his brother in New York. He always felt happy when that time came around. It seemed almost like an annual tradition. Jerome had already resolved, in his mind, that whenever his father passed away, he would leave the priesthood in search of his dream, fulfilling his dream. He knew he had enough time.

But then, suddenly, there were sweeping changes in the church brought about by changes in the judicial system. These changes could railroad Fr. Jerome's plans for the future, His life would never be the same and his future plans would indefinitely be on hold. The church had made a deal to turn over records of priests having sexual contact with minors in the past. This new law was pretty much along the lines as the statute for murder. The statute had no time limit. This directive came into being amidst a great outcry from the community, the result of numerous complaints by minors, mostly after they became adults, of sexual abuse by priests.

In the past, allegations were ignored and often swept under the rug. "Enough is enough" was the theme of a huge protest rally organized by some politicians and influential clergy members. It was meant to encourage victims to speak out.

Fr. Jerome's life would take a sudden and unexpected turn, because just one year after Jerome became an ordained priest, he had sexual relations with a fifteen year old female. It was called abuse. Abuse was a strong accusation since both parties admitted that the sex was consensual. Due to her age however, she could not legally give consent. The parents of the girl got word of this incident and threatened the church with a lawsuit. The church apologized to the parents and agreed to settle the matter out of court, with a stipulation that neither mother nor daughter would make this settlement public. This incident was kept a secret due to Father Thom's influence.

The church did compensate the family and they all walked away from the deal contented. The agreement was that nothing further of this incident was to be said and that no further legal action would be taken.

Now the question that plagued Fr. Jerome and the Diocese was if the agreement would hold well in the light of this new law.

These changes were of great concern to Fr. Jerome. He stood to lose everything if his father was forced in any way to follow church protocol, and surrender all past records of sexual abuse cases, involving minors. Jerome thought that now, more than ever, he needed to get rid of the records, which his father, as head of the Diocese had kept safely all these years. But first, Fr. Jerome thought he should speak to Fr. Thom. It would be nerve racking, after all these years, to speak about this topic, but it seemed important to discuss these things with his Dad. Fr. Jerome spent many sleepless nights pondering his best approach to this volatile situation.

They hardly knew where Cindy was living now. Word had it that a year or two after the settlement, they had moved to Albany, in upstate New York, approximately 200 miles north of New York City. Many times, in his quiet moments these days, Jerome found himself thinking of Cindy. I wonder what became of her. I guess she is probably married by this time, with a family of her own, he thought.

Even though Jerome was worried about what the outcome of this situation would be, he tried to convince himself that everything would be fine, if only he had faith. Sometimes he would say a prayer, and often the prayers did make him feel better. This new sexual abuse development was aired on radio and television nationwide. The Attorney General and District Attorneys, state by state, were encouraging victims to come forward.

Fr. Jerome always felt sick to think what a mess he had gotten himself into. This problem was of great concern since more and more the problems seemed to resurface. No matter what the Diocese did, Jerome knew a lot had to do with the way his father handled things. A lot depended on the way Fr. Thom handled Cindy.

Jerome was pretty sure that any day, the Attorney General of Massachusetts was going to hear from Cindy and come knocking at his door, so to speak. Fr. Jerome felt sick to his stomach, hoping Cindy would contact the Diocese first. He kept wondering if and when his day was going to come.

He was certainly not looking forward to that day. And he no longer watched the news. Since the announcement was made, quite a number of priests were being led away in handcuffs, accused of rape, sodomy and having carnal knowledge of minors. Jerome could just picture himself in a similar situation on the six o'clock news.

The right thing to do was to surrender this information to the relevant authorities. The church must honor its agreement, with no exception. Jerome kept thinking more and more of this situation and it seemed as though his father read his thoughts.
Fr. Thom came to him one day and said, "Son, something very important has come up. We need to talk."

Fr. Jerome froze immediately, even though he pretty much knew and anticipated what this very important something would be. But he could not acknowledge the full impact of what he was about to hear. Jerome hoped that it would be something different than what was foremost on his mind. His thoughts raced back in time to remember the last time that he and his father had a personal conversation, let alone to be summoned to his father's office. Father Thom beckoned Jerome into his office. "Cindy called me today." Then he waited agonizingly for what seemed to be an eternity, before he continued.

"She said she heard the good news that victims of any sex abuse by a priest should call the authorities and that she was going to report this incident, if we did not, despite our agreement."

Fr. Jerome was immediately transformed into a fit of rage. He became flushed. His facial expression changed, from anger to excitement, followed by fear. Jerome's thoughts raced back to the affair they had. He knew after the first time it happened he should have been strong and refused to let it go on and on until they were caught in the act.

Nearly two and a half minutes went by before Jerome could regain his composure and return to the thread of the conversation. His only response was "Dad, did you get her phone number?"

"No, but she has promised to call back within a few days."

"Father!!!" Jerome blurted out "When she calls again, you need to let me handle this." He thought to himself that it was a pity that the church did not have caller id. The cheap bastards would never want to pay for it.

Fr. Jerome went on, "What is it she wants from us after all this time?"

"At the moment things seem unclear, but one can only imagine more money or perhaps revenge." Revenge should never be a factor, unless all along her plan was to get Jerome and the church for her personal gains. It seemed farfetched that a kid of fifteen would be thinking that far ahead to have such an elaborate scheme to deceive the Church. But Fr. Jerome was continually surprised at the extent some people would go for material gains.

He continued, "There can be no thought of revenge when Cindy was the one who initiated this situation in the first place. Revenge is for people who were taken advantage of. In a sense I did, because of her age, yet on the other hand she insisted on doing what was done. Father, I have asked for forgiveness a thousand times or more. I have relived this nightmare over and over. There has not been a day that goes by that I don't remember my actions, with regret and remorse.

"The more I think about this mess, the more convinced I am that this was a setup. She purposely did what she did in order to blackmail us. It is difficult to fathom a plot of this magnitude without an adult being behind all of this."

Father Thom saw his chance to cut in and said, "Then, as if nothing mattered, you played right into their hands, they played you like a violin. Your actions were not like that of a priest. Your actions were irresponsible. You acted like the others that are being brought up on charges and now, will ultimately no longer be able to continue in the priesthood since they will have to be registered sex offenders."

Jerome replied, "Father, what bothers me the most is the extent people would go to for money, just for material gains. Now my life is ruined by a little blackmailer. I tried on numerous occasions to even avoid her, to the extent that she became aware of my effort. Even back then, I knew what the ramifications would be. This situation now comes back to haunt me. I tried my best, for as long as I could, to avoid this happening because I knew what I would be in for, and then something overcame me eventually."

Jerome remembered that he had succumbed to the temptation right after returning from his vacation time of wild parties and wild women, in New York. Fr. Jerome never wanted his father to know the reason why he always looked forward to spending his vacation with Ray. Jerome said, "My dear father, my best option would be to find her and convince her that we did make an agreement which obligates her to keep her silence."

More like physically persuade her was what Jerome really had in mind. Maybe let her disappear forever. "Father, this is something I was not looking forward to, and ever since that announcement came, I have been having mixed feelings about this subject." Jerome knew full well that there was no end to blackmail, and the only solution was to get rid of the blackmailer.

Fr. Thom did not tell Jerome that he also had skeletons in his closet that he wanted to get rid of, to clear his own conscience. How to go about it was the biggest problem.

Fr. Thom's conscience was bothering him, yet he thought he owed it to himself to continue to keep his own secret under wraps, forever, if possible. These new changes were wreaking havoc in the minds of many priests. It was a great ethical dilemma for the head of the Diocese, to choose between his son being disgraced and charged for statutory rape, and his own situation. Last, but not least, the church's ethics had to be upheld. However, Jerome was not the only one with his share of problems; Fr. Thom had problems of his own.

Fortunately, for the old priest, Jerome was not aware of his father's problem. Fr. Jerome's situation was a closely kept secret between father and son. In the light of the prevailing circumstances for these two priests, self- preservation was foremost in their minds. Father Thom knew that his own personal situation was nothing compared to his son's. Despite the fact that he (Fr. Thom) had used the church funds to cover up his wrong doings, and could face embezzlement charges, Fr Thom knew that most Dioceses operated by trust and audits were rare, except for questionable financial transactions. The church had no knowledge that Fr. Thom had used funds belonging to the institution for his own benefit. His hope was that it would not be discovered while he was alive. Fr. Thom had embezzled funds from the church while he was married and held office as a treasurer to the Diocese. Once he was elected head of the Diocese he destroyed the evidence of his wrong doings.

Fr. Thom had been accused of fathering a child out of wedlock. He was not quite sure if the child was his but he decided to quiet the scandal none the less. He embezzled funds to quiet the scandal and, had it not been for blackmail, Fr. Thom's hands would have been clean. That was one part of Fr. Thom's woes taken care of. What if the mother of the child should decide she needed to blackmail him again?

Father Thom was more mindful of what a scandal would do to his position. He felt pretty sure that if he could hold onto his position as head of the Diocese, his son would be safe. The worst that could happen is that he could lose his position as the head priest but the church would never make the embezzlement public. He knew for sure that he would have to keep his position at the top, at all cost, in order to protect his son. Fr. Thom realized that the safety and well being of both father and son were contingent on him retaining his position, yet he knew in order to maintain his position, it would be costly. Right after his installation as head of the Diocese, his so called baby's mother resurfaced. He had to pay her again for her silence. He knew better than anyone else where his son was coming from when he called Cindy a blackmailer.

There was a lot more the old Priest knew that Fr. Jerome did not have even the slightest idea about. For that reason Fr. Thom knew he had to keep things under his control. Many priests had strongly opposed his appointment to that highly esteemed position, in light of the fact that Fr. Thom had left the ministry for longer than five years before returning.

This was one of the times when Jerome had regrets that he was a priest because his thoughts surprised him. He had evil thoughts and intentions for both his father and Cindy, and he whispered a prayer for forgiveness. Then, Fr. Jerome continued his dialogue with his father in a more normal tone. Jerome knew that he had to think and think fast. At first he thought he should leave the Diocese and seek refuge with his brother Ray, but then that would not resolve things. His second thought was to find Cindy and try to work something out. But how could he go about doing something of that nature. First of all, he didn't know where she was living. Then even if he knew where to find her, what would his plan be? What would be the best approach?

Even when all these questions were answered in his mind, Jerome knew that what he had to do would take time, and he did not have the time or the money. He also knew he could not leave the diocese for any length of time because he had already had his vacation for the year. When Jerome thought about money, his anger resurfaced and for the first time he entertained the evil thought that a little while earlier had entered his head. He knew there would be only one way to take care of a blackmailer.

The second option in this instance "going to the police" was out of the question. The last thing in the world he wanted was his secret to be exposed. He had his pride and his responsibility to uphold, let alone to be embarrassed in public by the media. The thought of imprisonment was very daunting. He figured there could be only one option. Ray would have the contact for what he was thinking about but in order for him to help, he would have to know Jerome's closely guarded secret.

Weeks turned into months and Fr. Jerome's agony was just starting to subside when his father once again summoned him to another meeting.

"She called," was all Fr. Thom said, and then sat back.

"What did she say?" Jerome asked out loud and, in his mind, one thousand times.

"What did Cindy say, dad?"

"She said that she would like some more money, a sum of money, this time, more than double the settlement. She then went on to laugh and say her funds from the previous settlement went to her mother, because of her age and the money had already been exhausted."

More than ever, her resolve was to be paid a huge sum of money or Fr. Jerome was to be behind bars. Cindy was out to get what she could from the deal. At the time of the settlement, Cindy was only fifteen. This is blackmail, Jerome said to himself and this is more than Jerome could handle at this time. He told his father he needed time away from the Diocese to concentrate on his next step.

The following day Fr. Jerome departed for New York.

CHAPTER TWO

Late September into early October was the most vulnerable time in Cindy's life. Events over the past five years had shaped it that way. The beautiful colors associated with fall, the falling leaves, the exotic sceneries, were as though Mother Nature turns our attention to the holiday season ahead, with an abundant array of beautiful things. The fresh atmosphere brings to mind the calm serenity that follows the sweltering summer heat. In the winter months, everything seems to slow down. Fall and winter seem like a time to hibernate, a time to sit back and take stock of the past and what's in store for the future.

At least that was Cindy's perception of the latter months. Maybe taking stock was the cause for her depression. Thoughts of the concluding year as well as the anticipation of the New Year. Maybe love, romance and that important failed resolution that only lasted the first three weeks of the then New Year. Now comes rolling back into focus the feeling of anticipation for the holidays, Halloween, Thanksgiving and Christmas.

The thought of millions of families spending time together; memories of the first Christmas she spent married to her first love; thoughts of families spending time huddled up around the fire-place, watching their favorite television shows. The men in particular, always seemed to watch football. As though the real manly thing to do is to watch the ball game. As the women significantly bond together to spend quality time shopping, as the apparent, dazed husbands/ boyfriends converge around the television set. The women already know that they would not be able to get their other half's attention for maybe the next four to six hours anyway. This was the time smart women asked their spouse for extra funds to go shopping and got it from their dazed partners, especially Super Bowl Sunday.

Fall, to some extent, should be a happy time for Cindy, maybe if she had the family support system to comfort and support her when daylight saving time turned her world into darkness at four thirty pm. Cindy wished she knew where her mother was. Being an only child, she had no one close to turn to. The thought of another long cold winter weighed heavily on her mind. It was under these same circumstances three years earlier when Cindy met and married Wayne. To be precise, they met in February then became an item in March and got married six months later. At that time Cindy did have misgivings about Wayne but the thought of spending another long cold winter alone, got the better of her judgment. Cindy thought love would conquer all. Things went well for a time. Wayne was the perfect gentleman, telling Cindy all that a woman would want to hear. But once Cindy became pregnant, Wayne began spending more and more time away on business. At first Wayne told her he had an internet business in Florida, then he was a real estate salesman, so he went to work when he wanted. Cindy was never curious because he always had enough money to satisfy her shopping crave. Her marriage to Wayne lasted for three years. The longer their marriage lasted the less Cindy saw of Wayne. One year before their eventual separation and divorce, Cindy gave birth to a stillborn baby on Halloween night.

The loss of her baby seemed to be a strain on their marriage because Wayne wanted to have children of his own. He accused Cindy of attempting an abortion at the beginning of her pregnancy and blamed her for the death of his son. Cindy denied vehemently and offered to take a lie detector test. Cindy knew that Wayne was using the situation as an excuse for his shortcomings.

A year later, in early December, just when it seemed they would get back together despite being divorced, Wayne was shot execution style.

The Deadly Priest

CHAPTER THREE

The loss of her child and subsequently her ex-husband was much more than Cindy ever thought she could bear. She went into a deep depression and almost became suicidal. This was the reason why Cindy dreaded fall and winter so much. The memories, the long, cold, lonely days and sleepless nights, the thought of spending another lonely winter, all but drove Cindy to the brink of suicide.

Though many looked forward to Halloween, Thanksgiving and Christmas to herald the end of another year and to welcome the New Year, this was the time Cindy dreaded most because it brought back painful memories, memories she would have with her for the rest of her life. It was always this time of year, especially Halloween that she felt the worst.

Cindy was looking forward to the great event of child bearing, the greatest miracle of all, the miracle of giving birth. Only to find out that her first born, a boy had not survived childbirth, Cindy was sad, angry and depressed all at the same time. Two years later, the memories remained fresh in Cindy's mind as though it had happened yesterday. No amount of therapy had been able to erase the memory of that

Halloween night. After the doctor told her the bad news, those words stayed fresh in her mind for a long time.

Cindy had yet another reason for her distaste for the latter months of the year. For almost one full year after her ex-husband's death, she was considered a person of interest. It took the cops nearly one year to establish her innocence. Wayne was not the real estate agent he led her to believe, neither did he own an internet business in Florida. In fact, Wayne was a drug dealer. Their story book courtship and marriage had come to a screeching halt when she found out that, not only did he lie to her, but that his frequent trips to Florida were simply to visit and sleep with his mistress.

This made her furious and she immediately filed for divorce. "No wonder he never wanted me to travel with him on his supposed business trips," she thought. Wayne did try to make amends to Cindy for his deceit, even after their divorce proceedings became final. He began spending more time with Cindy. Things started to look promising. No more trips to Florida by himself. Wayne now took Cindy everywhere he went. He even took her to Florida, but that effort would be his fatal mistake. As Cindy considered whether she would give her romance another chance, Wayne was killed.

His former mistress had him killed. Evidence came out at trial of a murder for hire scheme, in his ex-mistress trial. She was sentenced to thirty years. Her hit man got life without parole. Cindy was bitter and swore to stop at nothing for revenge. It was bittersweet. Cindy was happy to be vindicated, but furious with herself for being so naive to believe Wayne.

It was also late summer that she last heard from her mother. Cindy remained hopeful that her mother was still alive, even though her whereabouts remained a mystery. "Where is my mother when I need her?" She thought the loss of her first born boy child was devastating. If only the circumstances could have been different. If she could change the past, or change other things, perhaps in her world there might not be autumn or winter, perhaps just spring and summer. Early spring especially, when one had the whole year ahead of them rather than to have to face the memory of a loss at the cold dark end of the year.

Spring would definitely be her favorite time of the year. The days seem brighter, flowers blooming, birds chirping, the air seems fresh and free. The mind is filled with the feelings of expectation and anticipation of what the New Year has in store. Then if it didn't happen by spring, there is always summer to look forward to, another of Cindy's favorite times of year. Summer following right on the heels of spring to her was even better, so much to do, travel, vacations, cookouts, barbeques, family reunions, picnics, etc.

There is so much to do when the weather is warm. Outdoor activities always seemed to keep Cindy's mind off thoughts of the past.

It never occurred to her after all these years that, by mid February, things usually seemed to get better for her. Also thoughts of Wayne at this time were heavy on her mind because it was in this same time frame when she was introduced to him. It was love at first sight for Cindy. Their relationship blossomed into marriage and, despite their eventual divorce, Cindy always thought about him, especially around this time of year.

Those events made a big impact in Cindy's life. Now, her thoughts suddenly turned to Jerome. It was also fall when she was caught in the act with him. Looking back now, she really did not care because now she was going to benefit from that illicit action. Thoughts of those events came to her. Cindy knew, within herself, that Fr. Jerome was not one hundred percent to blame.

Young as she was, she very much wanted it to happen and it could be safely said that she initiated the contact in a big way. It was by no means the first time when they were caught. That is why she was somewhat reluctant to go to the authorities in the first place.

Cindy did keep her affair with Jerome a secret from Wayne with the aid of a therapist. Now she felt guilty that she had never told her husband what had happened in her past. But as her therapist had said, Wayne may have wanted to pursue the matter and take things into his own hands. Now, more than ever, Cindy kept remembering what she was told by her therapist. She must put aside her fears and confront the perpetrator.

As of yet, she did not think she was ready to face such a situation. She knew that only she and Fr. Jerome knew the real facts of the matter. She could actually visualize what his response would be. It was never her intention to confront the priest for she knew it would be difficult to face Jerome. In the guise of a rape victim, Cindy was old enough to know Jerome had not raped her. She knew that she was to blame for initiating the sexual contact, in other words, the sex was consensual, the only problem being that she was then a minor and as such could not give consent. Cindy had no intention of reporting this incident to the authorities. Instead she saw this as an opportunity to exploit the situation and reap financial rewards.

In late November, Cindy got home after working a double shift, sixteen long hours. She was cold and drained. The weather was bad, so Cindy was looking forward to a warm bath and a movie to relax and unwind, before going to bed. But first she had to stop at the convenience store, and video store to pick up a few items, and at the same time call the Diocese.

To her recollection, it had been nearly three months since she had last called. The phone at the Diocese rang but no one answered. She tried again, but this time she received a busy signal. She decided to complete her shopping then give it one last shot. She tried again, but still no answer.

On her way home she thought to herself that something was not right. Fr. Thom always picked up the phone on the first or second ring each time she called. Maybe the stress and strain of her calls had done something to him. Or maybe he would no longer take her calls, she thought to herself. Cindy was not aware that the church did not have caller ID.

"Maybe I should speak to Jerome himself, after all,"

she thought to herself.

It took her another three weeks before she learned that the old priest had been hospitalized with a heart attack and that Jerome was being transferred from Massachusetts, to another Parish not yet decided or announced.

"I will have to implement plan B," she thought.

Father Jerome returned to the Diocese after spending only a few hours in the Big Apple. It turned out that his brother Ray was in trouble of some sort and had left his home in a hurry, to "cool" things off, leaving no forwarding address. Jerome having nowhere to stay, spent a few quality hours in a popular bar he and his brother frequented. He stayed in the bar until ten pm, by which time he made friends with a prostitute and spent a few hours at her place. He left on the next available greyhound bus bound for Massachusetts.

It seemed that some luck was on Jerome's side. The bar he had visited and left forty-five minutes earlier, was the favorite hangout spot for two patrons known as Marble and Scar, whom unknowingly to Jerome, were pursuing his brother to enforce a collection debt. They were regulars at that bar, as was Ray. The Duo kept order at the bar for drinks, often times throwing out disorderly drunks. The bartender always loved when the thugs were present because patrons had to be orderly or risk being thrown out bodily. Jerome and Ray frequented the bar when they were together. Marble and Scar had missed their connecting flight from Las Vegas to New York, via Philadelphia, due to bad weather. Fortunately for Jerome, they had just missed him at the bar. The thugs were returning from their search for Ray and indulged in some gambling at the same time. The expenses of their trip would be added to Ray's tab.

Jerome was not aware of the danger that loomed over his head, for if the thugs had laid eyes on him no questions would have been asked. Ray and Jerome were identical twins and the two thugs would not have listened to what he had to say, for sure they would not ask him for his ID. All they knew was what Ray looked like and they wanted him bad. The thugs learned of Jerome's presence and left immediately in search of the prostitute he had befriended. Fortunately for her, she never made it a point to broadcast to everyone in the bar where she lived. She left that strictly to paying customers. Rumor had it that Ray had borrowed money from a loan shark and was finding it difficult to keep up with his payment schedule.

The loan shark sent the two thugs, Minton, nicknamed Marble, because he had a marble eye and Chuck, nicknamed Scar Face, because he had a scar down his face from his forehead to his chin. Word on the street had gotten to Ray that those two dangerous men were looking for him, so Ray split. He knew the reputation of those two guys and knew he would be no match for one, let alone two. Minton and Chuck always worked together after their release from the Penitentiary.

When they met in the pen, Minton was doing time for a bank heist and was on the last few months of his seven year sentence. Chuck was released a few months later on good behavior. He did three years for assault and battery committed during a card game. He had seriously injured a friend for cheating at cards. The card cheater was hospitalized and spent more than three months in a coma. Ever since the two got out of the pen, they had become inseparable, pulling off enforcement jobs for loan sharks/the mob. Ray knew them well from the bar they frequented and saw what they were capable of doing.

They both had long rap sheets dating back to their juvenile days from aggravated assault, shoplifting, burglary, attempted murder, racketeering, money laundering and attempted rape. Assault and battery in every degree possible, assault and battery was Chuck's favorite. The two thugs were now contracted for enforcement of loan defaults and were finding it a pleasure hurting defaulters and being paid for hurting people. It was a plus for them, icing on the cake.

Two weeks later, after Jerome's brief vacation in the Big Apple, Cindy returned to work to find a business card from a private investigator requesting her to call him about a matter of extreme importance. She immediately went back out to the pay phone and called the Diocese. To her surprise, Fr. Jerome answered. For a moment she did not know what to say but quickly collected herself and decided to pretend to be a church member. "I'm calling to find out how Fr. Thom is doing" she made it sound honest and natural, even though she was tempted to say how is my father doing but resisted the urge. "Is he still in the hospital?" she asked.

Cindy was told by her mother that Fr. Thom might be her father, only after the incident with Jerome but her mother made her swear to tell no one, not even Jerome. Cindy remained hopeful that one day before the old priest died she would know the truth. Cindy grew up thinking her stepfather was in fact her biological father. The more Cindy thought about this whole situation the more confusing she was becoming these days. Since she learned about Fr. Thom's secret relationship with her mother, the whole situation was reading like a Jerry Springer show but Cindy didn't dare go there. Would Springer say "Fr. Thom, are you not the Father?"

Thoughts of incest, passed through her mind. Maybe that was why she thought she loved Fr. Jerome in a special way. Was he, or was he not her brother? The question played with her mind. But, if indeed he was her brother, she couldn't make him go to jail. Cindy thought of the embarrassment this entire situation would cause if the media should get hold of the truth. A brother and sister having sex. More than likely Jerome was unaware of the possibility he was her brother. Cindy's thoughts were back on track as Jerome responded "He's under doctor's care at home and cannot speak on the phone."

Cindy really wanted to find out why they had sent a private investigator to her job. But she didn't dare ask Jerome for fear she might confirm her identity and location by the telephone area code. Jerome said "Madam, I did not catch your name." Cindy stuttered "My name is Jane" and hung up before Jerome could say another word. Was it fear, embarrassment, anger or all of the above? Those questions were difficult for even Cindy herself to answer.

Cindy did not return to work. Neither did she call Hector, the private investigator. She stayed at her best friend Jasmine's house, thinking and pondering her next move. Her biggest concern was whether Jerome was on to her since he was being transferred or if Hector, was indeed a private investigator or a cop. She knew that extortion was a crime and she also knew she was blackmailing the Diocese.

Finally, after a few days, Cindy decided that she should leave Albany for fear of being prosecuted and imprisoned. She remembered what a close shave she had with the detectives when her husband was killed because she had no alibi. Despite having a rough life, Cindy had never had problems with the law, except for receiving a citation once for driving without a license. There were times when she gave prostitution a thought but could never bring herself to fully exploit her thoughts. That was also before she met her husband. This was the only brush Cindy had with the law. She was questioned at length about the death of her husband but was never held in custody. She was considered a prime suspect, until the investigation revealed a murder for hire plot.

Ray called Jerome and said that he was en route to the Diocese to see his ailing father, and would spend a few days there. Ray intended to spend as long as possible, maybe a month or two, depending on the situation in New York. He knew the thugs would come after him, regardless of where he went.

Both Fr. Thom and Fr. Jerome were delighted to see Ray. Jerome was especially happy because he felt that if there was one person in this world who could help his cause, it would have to be his twin brother Ray. Jerome, in desperation, decided that he had no other choice but to tell Ray of his troubles from the beginning to the end. First he wanted to find out, in a subtle way, what kind of trouble Ray was in and if Ray could be of help before confiding in him. In some way, Jerome felt embarrassed about the situation even though Ray had been aware that his priestly brother was no saint. Jerome felt comfortable doing what he did away from the Diocese and away from the eyes of his parishioners. Within himself, it was difficult to determine if he was embarrassed because of Cindy's age or because he got caught red handed.

These days, his thoughts were killing him so he turned his attention to his brother Ray. Jerome had the premonition that Ray was running from trouble rather than being concerned with his father's health. Jerome decided he would not let Ray know that he was in New York a week or so earlier. At least not right away. On the other hand since leaving New York, Ray had not contacted anyone there so he was not aware of his brother's brief visit.

Ray was not eager to discuss his past. Ray knew that Jerome was in some sort of trouble a few years ago but he had never learned its nature. So went the game of cat and mouse between the two brothers. The only thing short in that room, was a deck of cards.

The Deadly Priest

CHAPTER FOUR

Jerome finally decided that, since he was in hot water and needed his brother's assistance, he would be the one to break the ice. After dinner and after making the old man comfortable, Jerome took Ray to the conference room and opened a bottle of his father's best imported scotch whisky.

Jerome began, "My brother, I am indeed happy to see you. More so, I would have been even happier under different circumstances. I do know right now that we are both in some sort of trouble or the other. Despite the fact that I am a priest, I now find myself in troubling times. You know the sermon we preach, 'whatsoever a man sow that shall he reap'?

"Well, I sowed my seed of destruction eleven years ago, as you should know by now. Wine, women and song were my thing back then, even after I was ordained a priest. You know as well as I do, I went into the Priesthood to please my father. Had I not gone this way I would not have anywhere to live. I never thought I would be capable of surviving in a big city like you did. You have certainly made a name for yourself down there. I should have listened to you rather than to Dad. Now, I must tell you what my problem is, but first I must let you know that I know that you are also in some type of trouble."

Ray's jaw dropped, he said, "I am only here to see dad."

Jerome replied, "Would you believe me if I told you that bad news travels fast?"

Now it was Jerome's time to lie, "Ray", Jerome said, "I was in New York last week. On account of the old man's illness and his inability to travel I went to a three day conference on his behalf and I decided to give you a surprise check. But you surprised me. It was as though you had moved to another city. Your friends were hesitant at first to let me know that you were in some sort of mess, until I told them I would wait until you returned. They said they would not advise me to hang around the bar, since they did not know if you would return for a few days or even weeks.

"They also said that, since we are identical twins, they thought that it would be in my best interest (priest or not) to leave at the earliest opportunity for fear of a mistaken identity situation. I did not need to be told twice. I left there as soon as I could."

Jerome stopped speaking briefly to have a drink and thought to himself it was time to hear from Ray.

"Do you need to know more or are you willing to let us know if we will be in any danger by having you stay here?" Ray decided to tell his woes but not before he heard Jerome's story.

At first, Jerome decided to play it slick and described the incident with Cindy as a scandal. But, as he went on, he thought it best to level with his brother truthfully but did not elaborate until the scotch got the better of him. He simply told his brother about Cindy and the fact that she had a crush on him and that one day an elder came by and caught them in the act of having sex. It was not the first time they had sex in the Diocese. He related how the matter was reported to Father Thom, and Cindy's parents were notified. A few weeks later, the parents of Cindy suggested they take the matter to the authorities. Fr. Thom asked them if there could be any other way to resolve this matter? Cindy's mother, Olga, jumped at the idea. At the time Cindy's mother and boyfriend were crack addicts, so the two sides reached an amicable settlement of $15,000.00. Nothing further was to be said.

Ray interjected "I know the rest!!! She or her parents are blackmailing you."

Jerome was amazed but not quite surprised at Ray's response. Ray added "it happens all the time", especially since the Attorney General made the announcement calling for minors to come forward, and report priests.

"I have heard about this and was hoping you or Dad had no skeletons in the closet."

"Do you know that it is rumored that Dad could be Cindy's biological Father?" Jerome was stung by Ray's response but quickly regained his composure. Ray continued before Jerome could respond. "Now I am hearing you are in a worse bind than Dad. The worst that can happen to him is that he loses his position as head of the Diocese."

Jerome could take it no longer he blurted out. "Then where does that leave me, Ray, wide out in the open?" Jerome was both annoyed and angry with his brother for spelling out the facts. Jerome never wanted to know that Cindy could possibly be his sister. This angered him even more. Jerome had also heard that rumor many years ago but never took it seriously. As a matter of fact, Father Thom denied paternity vehemently and Jerome believed him to the point that he almost forgot about that allegation until Ray brought it up again.

"This is something big" Ray continued. "I have seen priests taken away in handcuffs for sexual acts done longer than ten years back, in most cases to boys who have become grown responsible adults."

"Well", said Jerome, "Cindy was fifteen at the time so she did not benefit from the cash. She's now under the assumption that she should get a piece of the pie. She would like to have three times the fifteen thousand settlement, her mother got on her behalf. From what I understand, she is not doing so great in Albany, working a nine to five job, waiting in a restaurant for minimum wages. She calls dad from time to time, but her demands so far are unclear. Ray, what do you suggest?"

"Well, Jerome, I might be able to take care of that problem for you. The details I will have to work out after I make a few phone calls."

"So let's hear your troubles, Ray," was Jerome's next response. Ray was hesitant at first, never wanting Jerome to know he was right. Eventually he succumbed to Jerome's fixed stare.

"Well, when you said you knew I was in trouble you were right, I didn't come here for the sole purpose of seeing Dad. I came because I wanted things to cool off a little. I can tell you I am not in trouble with the law, but it might be better that I was in trouble with the law than the mess I have found myself in. My dear brother, you have been to New York on numerous occasions and you have seen my lifestyle, whores, pimps, drugs, gays, lesbians. My number one love to the extent of compulsion, is gambling. In other words I'm a compulsive gambler. I borrowed money from loan sharks from time to time, when things were not so good. The first six months of this year my tally was thirty-five grand. A few days later I took in ten grand from gaming and my drug business.

"Apparently the loan shark needed a minimum of twenty thousand within three days and the pressure was coming down on me. Rather than applying pressure to my faithful customers and dealers, I decided to split, taking with me eight grand. I did not pay him any of what I owed him. My first stop was Atlantic City where I lost two grand playing black jack."

I then went to the Indian reservation in Connecticut were I lost another two thousand. I was down to four thousand cash in hand, so since my luck was not running well on the East Coast, I decided to try Vegas. I did well for a few days but when I was left with two thousand I decided to visit Dad.

"So what about the loan shark?", asked Jerome.

"Word is he is looking for me, so the longer I take to return the cash the worse the situation gets."

"So what do you plan to do now?"

"I'm just hoping to relax here for a while before deciding my next move. For sure, I really can't go back there without his money. My dilemma is the longer I stay away, the more his interest grows. Invariably, in most instances, the interest becomes greater than the principle. That is loan sharking for you! So, since my luck is running out, I guess I will not return there soon. Word was the loan shark's boys were in Vegas looking for me. As a matter of fact, I came close to bumping into them at a strip joint. That's when I decided to leave Vegas for a while and come here. I am sure by now they are back in New York. I will call John to find out."

CHAPTER FIVE

Ray returned to Las Vegas, after spending just seven days with his brother and father at the Diocese. He promised to keep in close contact but could not stand the peace, serenity and quiet of the Diocese.

He did well on the first day he arrived in Vegas, ending the day with five thousand dollars. The second day was cloudy. He lost four thousand in less than four hours. He called Jerome, hoping to lift his spirits and told him about his winnings the previous day, but did not mention how badly he did on day two. Jerome felt encouraged and for the first time felt sure that Ray would be able to deliver him out of this situation. Jerome thought to himself that, had he listened to Ray in the first place, he might not be in the mess he now found himself in.

Cindy jumped on the first bus out of Albany. Somehow, she felt that Jerome was on to her. She felt she had to leave. Cindy had a hunch that Jerome would stop at nothing to make sure he was not convicted of sexual assault of a minor. Cindy had purchased her tickets using her friend Jasmine's credit card and identity. She would take no chances. She took every precaution to cover her tracks. Cindy was New York City bound and it would be her first trip to the Big Apple. It was something she had long wanted to do, spending a good many years of her life dreaming of visiting the greatest city in the world and often wondering what it would be like for her.

Cindy's thoughts centered on her first day in New York. What would it be like? All thoughts were now on the Big Apple, the bright lights, the bars, the Statue of Liberty, museums, the zoo and other places of interest not to forget the night life. So many clubs and the fact that the city never sleeps. Cindy even forgot for the time being, about her distant relative living in the Bronx. She hoped that with the little money she had she would be able to spend a few days in a motel and try to locate this relative. She dyed her hair blonde and decided to pose as a school teacher. She arrived safely in New York, via a greyhound bus, checked into a motel and began her search. Days turned into weeks and she could not find the relative she was looking for. Coming from a small town she never envisioned what a big city was like. Before her arrival in the Big Apple she was pretty sure she would find her relative.

She even visited the library and posted an ad on the internet and also did the same in a local newspaper. After awhile Cindy knew it would be difficult. Three weeks later Cindy found herself running low on cash and once again decided to call the Diocese. The Diocese was becoming her ATM machine. Fr. Thom answered, she told him she was desperate for money and demanded that he wire her some money via Western Union to New York City.

This was the break Fr. Jerome was waiting for. He

had a burning desire to meet Cindy face to face. It seemed that his father was denying him the privilege to handle things his way. Jerome felt sure that his brother Ray would be able to find her. It seemed that she had played right into his hands. But first, Jerome must contact Ray and give him the good news. Even though in order for Ray to return to New York, he must settle his debt. It took Jerome several attempts after midnight before he located Ray. Ray was busy gambling. He told Jerome that he was doing well and would continue to take his chances on the crap table a little more. His luck was running out.

In the meantime, Ray promised his brother he would call ahead to New York and have a friend work on locating Cindy. He told his brother he had fifteen thousand dollars left and needed another five thousand before he could return to New York. The following day Ray lost ten thousand dollars. Once he was successful, he would return to New York pay off his debt, and then continue his search for Cindy. Jerome provided Ray with an accurate description of Cindy but he didn't know that she was no longer a brunette. She was a blonde. That would be the only thing Jerome got wrong with Cindy's description. With the information Jerome provided, a sketch artist could come close to exactly what Cindy looked like or she could easily be picked out of a police lineup just by his description.

Fr. Thom sent Cindy five hundred dollars, just two days before she thought of taking refuge in a homeless shelter. One week later, Cindy decided to call her friend, Jasmine in Albany, only to find out that the private investigator, Hector, wanted to see Cindy in connection with a missing person he was trying to locate. It suddenly dawned on her that his appearance had nothing to do with the Diocese, if he could be taken at his word. When she last spoke to Fr. Thom, he was totally clueless about the private investigator. He told her that he wished he could shed some light on this new development but he was totally unaware of the circumstances. Fr. Thom expressed concern for her safety and told her to keep him informed about this new development. He sounded sincere so she believed him.

Fr. Thom suspected that Jerome was behind this private investigator and questioned Ray's sudden visit to the Diocese as well as Jerome's frequent disappearances. Fr. Thom was really concerned for her safety and would put nothing past Jerome these days. The priest had no doubt that his son would stop at nothing to do harm or see harm done to Cindy so that this problem would go away. Ray being in the picture, made the old priest even more suspicious. He knew well that Ray, for the most part, was never up to any good. Ray had always attracted trouble. The old priest was overly suspicious that his two sons had something to do with the visit of a investigator to Cindy's job.

In the meantime, due to her financial situation, Cindy knew it was time to return home, despite her circumstances. She had no choice but to return home or get a job in New York. Cindy wanted to stay in Albany just in case she got word of her missing mother. She wanted to be there in Albany where she was well known. Also, coming from a small town, she did not think she could cope with the really fast pace of big city life. Maybe not now. Maybe when she got some things in her mind resolved. For now, her missing mother would be number one on her list of priorities. Despite her mother's colorful past Cindy still thought, to find her mother one day would really be a gift from God. Cindy really needed her mother at this time, to confide in her about what was going on. She needed her paternity question answered, where are you now mother when I need you most? Cindy packed her belongings and headed home, never thinking to continue her search for the long lost relative in the Bronx.

Fr. Jerome really pictured his brother's life as interesting, enjoyable, exciting and intriguing. Speaking from a priest's point of view, where are his moral values? Jerome felt it was imperative that he should have a final showdown with his father for all the wrong things his father had done to his siblings and his mother, despite her illness. Not to mention Cindy's paternity fresh in his mind. Jerome's need for revenge pertained to his own doing, more than his family history. He felt his father was to blame. Somebody had to take the blame. Unfortunately, it is almost always the parent's fault. In Jerome's mind, if his mother was still alive, she would have to bear some of the blame. Irrationally, he thought it was his parents fault even if they tried to instill good morals and values sometimes. It would be said, "They were too strict." You can never win, no matter how hard you try to be a good parent.

Jerome decided that, once Cindy was located, he

would most certainly deal with her, regardless of his father's apparent feelings for her. Jerome sensed that his father had a soft spot for her and it was difficult for Jerome to understand at first. But now the pieces were beginning to fall into place. In the meantime, Fr. Thom was drifting in and out of senility, Jerome thought it was one of his acts, or a game, at times he could not remember who Jerome was but always seemed to be in his right mind, when Cindy called, on any given day. He always seemed in touch with reality to prepare and preach his sermon whenever it was his time to deliver the sermon.

Jerome inquired of his father's Cardiologist if his heart condition could cause his senility or Alzheimer disease? The doctor told Jerome those diseases were never known to be linked, yet there could be other issues that could be a contributing factor for his apparent senility. The doctor told Jerome it was definitely an early sign of Alzheimer's disease and that when his father recovered from his heart attack and was a little stronger, he would refer him to a psychiatrist for further evaluation. Despite Fr. Thom's apparent senility, he would lament at length, on the wrongful, weak, act of Jerome that was bringing shame and disgrace to his Diocese.

Before now, Jerome had no proof of his father's infidelity. Even though he had some idea that his father was unfaithful to his mother when she was alive, he hadn't the slightest idea that his father had a child out of wedlock. But since Ray brought up the subject, it remained fresh in Jerome's mind and it seemed a serious possibility existed that Jerome and Cindy were brother and sister. This tormented him.

Fr. Thom had wanted a DNA test to be certain he was not Cindy's father, however, Cindy's mother, Olga, would have nothing to do with a test. Threatening to go public with his infidelity if he dared try, Olga had pulled off a big bluff. She dared not let her husband know that Cindy might not be his daughter. So Fr. Thom's hands were tied having no choice but to leave things as they were. Fr. Thom did not consider that Olga herself could not afford to let her husband find out about her indiscretion. His focus was to prevent himself from being publicly ridiculed and criticized, and more than likely losing his position as head of the Diocese. Jerome could not understand why his Father was so protective of Cindy. Maybe it was because Fr. Thom accepted Cindy as his daughter. Jerome was clearly right in thinking that his father favored Cindy for some unexplained reason. Despite the circumstances, Fr. Thom had developed a deep inner feeling for Cindy.

At times, he almost hated the circumstance surrounding her birth. At times, he hated the situation he found himself in. Often times, he directed his anger at Jerome, for compounding the problem. Not only was he being blackmailed by Olga which was his problem anyway without Cindy and Jerome's involvement with each other. But now Jerome was being blackmailed by Cindy, and the worst part of the deal, Fr. Thom would be in the center having to pay for both blackmails from the Church's funds. The blackmail was not the worst part. The fact that Fr. Jerome could do prison time was Fr. Thom's biggest concern.

Therefore, Fr. Thom's resolve was to see that no harm came to Cindy, for fear of her being his child. Jerome no longer cared that Cindy could possibly be his sister. He thought the whole situation through and concluded that it was his father's fault. He was becoming tired of hearing the same thing every day. His father lamented on his wrong doings. Now he felt better because he knew he had his ammunition and was a walking, ticking time bomb waiting for the right opportunity to explode. Considering his father's game, Jerome decided he would wait until his father had his psychiatric evaluation before confronting him. He was convinced it was a game his father was playing to protect Cindy.

Ray spent three sleepless nights thinking about the problems that he faced. With just five thousand dollars in hand, he decided to have a go at an illegal card game, which paid handsome dividends. At the end of the day he walked away from the poker game with fifteen thousand dollars. Now anxious to return to New York, he told himself he would make one more go at it the following day since he had done so well the previous day. The following day his luck was not that great at first, but in the end he added another ten thousand dollars to his coffers. So finally Ray could return home, he was grateful because at one point he had gone as low as five grand. He called Jerome with the happy news that he would soon be returning to New York. He now had more than enough money to pay off his debt or so he led Jerome to believe. Encouraged by his good fortune, Ray turned his thoughts on home.

Ray knew exactly what he would do once he arrived.

First, he would put his winnings in a locker at the airport. The next important item on his agenda was to pay his rent. He was away for almost two months. Then the third most important thing was to look for Cindy. Ray boarded the first available flight to New York. It was midnight in Vegas. Ray knew he would arrive in New York before noon. That would give him time to find out the word on the street since he had not spoken to his friends in a while.

Ray wanted time to make sure it was safe to return to his apartment. He called his buddy John who told him word on the street was that two thugs were looking for him and his apartment was not a safe place to be. John even told Ray the word was they were in Las Vegas in search of him. He stayed with John for two days, but by the end of day two, Ray became restless and around eleven pm he decided to visit a bar he had frequented many years ago. He left the money with John for safe keeping and he purposely avoided his regular spot for fear the thugs would be there. Also, people who knew him might spread the word that he was back in town. He bought a prostitute, a few drinks, spent a few more hours in another bar near his home, then eventually ventured home around three am. He was not drunk by any means but the drinks he had made him feel a little elated to be back in his regular stomping ground. His thoughts were constantly on the mob. He told himself that he would pay off his debt tomorrow and hopefully get those thugs off his back.

He arrived at his apartment finally, and everything looked normal from outside, he turned his key in the lock, opened the door, reached for the light switch, turned the light on and then realized that he had company. Ray knew he should have listened to that little voice inside that told him to retrieve the thirty-eight caliber gun he kept hidden in the courtyard. Now, it was too late and it was apparent that they had been living in his apartment, awaiting his return. Ray really didn't have to worry about eviction. He was not going to be evicted, either way you looked at it, because his rent had been paid by the two thugs.

Now Ray must pay. They appeared to be the meanest members on the planet, with a combined weight of over seven hundred pounds. Both were taller than six feet. More like miniature sumo wrestlers. Sitting there with guns drawn, it was obvious that they had rehearsed exactly what they had to say and do. Somehow it seemed routine, Marble Eye was the first to speak. He said, "Close the door son, we really would not like to disturb your neighbors." Marble Eye went on, "or should we say our neighbors." Ray thought of running because he realized no good would come out of this situation, but he was looking down the barrels of not one, but two German Lugers with silencers attached.

The thugs looked like they would use their guns if they had. They weren't there for a cocktail party. Ray stuttered, "I've got the money" then Marble Eye got up. He moved fast for a man his size and before Ray knew it, he was sprawled on the floor. Both men came at him like a tag team. Not uttering a word, they simply lifted him up above their heads, and then they just dropped him. Ray's head hit the floor with a thud and for a moment the lights faded. Ray was determined to remain conscious. However, that was not his option. Scar Face kicked him in the head and Ray's headlights went out.

Cindy arrived safely in Albany. She was still scared. She stayed indoors for the next two weeks to make sure no one was looking for her. She thought of inquiring about her job but decided against it. She was uncertain about her next move. Thinking perhaps that Hector might be looming around the corner or in the dark, Cindy did not want to have to deal with Hector.

After three weeks, Cindy thought she had enough of hiding. She called her job and the manager was willing to have her back after her brief leave of absence. Cindy paid her rent with what was left of the five hundred dollars Fr. Thomas had sent her. Just a few days remained before her next rent was due and Cindy was praising her lucky stars she was accepted back to work. After seven days on the job Hector appeared. One of Cindy's coworkers was the first to spot him.

He sat way off in the distance behind a decorative plant. Cindy became nervous and almost dropped her serving tray on the guest she was serving, when she was told of Hector's presence.

However, she was determined to face Hector, to put an end to this cat and mouse game, as well as to determine Hector's true identity if possible. Cindy walked over to Hector, and despite being nervous calmly said "I am Cindy and how can I help you?" Cindy thought she knew who the stranger was. It was not Hector. Despite the elaborate disguise she knew she was speaking to Fr. Jerome. This startled her a bit, but she would play it cool because she could not be one hundred percent certain. There was a great amount of anger within. There would be a lot of questions she would ask the old priest. The main question being, why had he sent Jerome after her?

Just in case the old priest had nothing to do with Jerome being here at her job, this would be an indication that desperation was setting in on the part of either or both priests. If in fact Fr. Thom had nothing to do with it, then Jerome's desperation was evident.

Ray gradually regained consciousness. At first, he thought he was dreaming that he was walking in the rain on a cold winter night. Then he soon realized his dream was in reality a nightmare. He saw Marble Eye standing over him with a bottle of cold water, sprinkling the liquid on his face. Then, before he could fully come to, he felt a sharp pain in his head and his ribs; this made him aware of what had taken place an hour ago. Ray now wished he had still been unconscious because once again, Scar Face went to work on him. He kicked him in his ribs a few times, just enough to make Ray want to get up. It seemed that they were trained in the art of torture. They also seemed to be enjoying every minute of the cruelty. Ray was not sure he would be able to stand. His legs felt weak but how much more could he endure? Scar

Face came behind him, picked him up by his armpits and held him while Marble Eye went to work punching him in his stomach.

Ray's only recourse was to lean on one leg and kick Marble Eye with all the strength he could muster. He caught Marble off guard and in his tender spot. Scar sent Ray flying across the room and they both came at him, but it seemed that Marble wanted Ray for himself this time. Ray could hardly stand. He tried his utmost to get on his feet but this time Marble dropped all of his three hundred and fifty pounds of bodyweight on him. Ray felt as though he was run over by a truck. Ray was six feet two inches tall but only weighed one hundred and ninety-five pounds. The telephone rang and the two thugs looked at each other, Ray was drifting in and out of consciousness. He didn't have the time or presence of mind, to reflect on his brother Jerome.

He did not even have a mind at all. Everything depended on his body's ability to deal with the trauma inflicted by the two goons. The fact that the phone call was from Jerome, really didn't matter. He needed the assistance of 911 in an urgent way. The phone call went unanswered. Jerome at the other end had the premonition that something was going wrong with his twin brother. It is said that some twins have Extra Sensory Perception and they can feel strongly when something is wrong with their twin, especially if they are being hurt or in imminent danger. Like a Psychic thing, Jerome was feeling that strong energy. He wondered, was he still in Vegas? Did he go back to New York?

Things were happening so fast these days it was becoming difficult to keep track of events. Jerome retraced his thoughts for a moment then he remembered that when he last spoke to Ray, he was about to board his plane bound for New York. More questions surfaced; did he try to contact me at the Diocese this week? Jerome knew he was not there to receive his brother's phone call even if he did call. Now he started to feel guilty, because he insisted that his brother stay in touch. Jerome had just decided to give him a call and at the same time, mention that Cindy was back in Albany.

However, he had no intention of telling Ray where he was last week and about his future plans, now that he had located Cindy disguised as Hector the PI. The fact that Olga could not be found, was somewhat disturbing to Jerome. His trip to Albany was intended to find Olga and have her answer some of the burning questions. Once he found it difficult to locate Olga he decided to check out Cindy. Thankfully, she was back in Albany or Jerome would not be able to find her in the big City. Jerome found her from the telephone directory. The rest was easy; he staked out her residence and followed her to her job.

Hector, the private investigator, explained to Cindy, that he was seeking information on a missing person report, for a person related to her ex-husband. He went on to explain that during his investigations, he had uncovered information that would be of value to Cindy. But first she had to pay him a fee of twenty-five hundred dollars. He promised her that the information was well worth more than the money. Cindy was stunned. Her thoughts raced to her

The Deadly Priest

missing mother and for the first time, the Diocese flashed across her mind. Were these two evil people in the guise of priests responsible for her mother's disappearance?

If Jerome could find out about my ex-husband, then go so far as to find me, then the possibility existed. She thought they might have something to do with her mother's sudden disappearance. The more she thought of this situation, the more the whole situation appeared suspicious. She reflected on their settlement and thought to herself, these two priests, it seems, would stop at nothing short of regaining the funds the Diocese had paid to her parents, as a settlement. Cindy wanted him to leave. She was convinced she was not speaking to any Private Investigator. She was speaking to THE DEADLY PRIEST.

Despite her burning desire for him to leave, Cindy wanted to know what he knew, so she tried to be a patient listener. In the end, when she could take it no more, she said to him "Do you have a business card?"

Hector gave her his card, she promised to call him when she had the money. Something about this meeting felt eerie, strange and funky to Cindy. I will call you when I get rich, she wanted to shout after him.

Jerome had a heavy heart. He could almost feel something was going wrong with his brother. He sensed the trouble his twin brother was in but dared not tell his father. The two thugs left Ray's apartment after the phone rang. It was the first time that the phone had rung in the past two months that they were in and out of the apartment. They had a brief discussion and thought it best to leave.

They stripped Ray of the five hundred dollars he had in his pocket and other valuables in his apartment. They promised to return in twenty-four hours to complete the debt collection. Ray vaguely heard the thugs leave while slipping in and out of consciousness. The pain he now felt was excruciating. That telephone call from his brother saved Ray's life. Jerome's premonition was right, something was wrong with his brother.

After "Hector" left, Cindy immediately called the Diocese, but this time asked to speak to Jerome. Cindy knew if Jerome was away from the Diocese he had to be Hector. She was so furious that she even put caution to the wind. In the past, she always avoided calling from the pay phone at her job. But now she could not wait to call. The number Hector had given her on his card, had to be the number to a pay phone at the Diocese. Cindy used the number she always used to call the Diocese. She asked to speak to Jerome and Fr. Thom told her he was at a church conference and he would not be returning for another three weeks. Figuring he could buy some time. Cindy was now convinced Hector was indeed Jerome, despite his disguise.

"Fr. Thom are you sure that he attended the conference as he was supposed to or are you just trying to cover the fact that you sent him here in search of me?" Fr. Thom was shocked. He did not know what to say but he tried to maintain a normal tone. "My child, I have no knowledge of what you are talking about."

"My Child" Cindy wished those words were real, Fr. Thom knew it was possible. Jerome could be anywhere because he was not sent to any church conference. He collected himself and responded, "All that I can tell you my child is Jerome is attending a conference in Frankfurt, Germany. I cannot vouch for his whereabouts, but that is where he is supposed to be representing this Diocese." Fr. Thom himself did not know Jerome's whereabouts. He would prefer if Jerome did not make contact with Cindy, let alone have any discussion with her. He feared they might compare notes since he was unaware if Cindy knew he might be her biological father.

"MY CHILD" those words sounded real to Cindy. But despite the soothing effect of those words, Cindy was still angry and upset. She still seemed to want to punish the Diocese now that the opportunity had presented itself. Cindy pressed on, "Fr. Thom please let Jerome know that he or his representatives, friends or associates should not make any further attempts to contact or bother me, or I will let the attorney general phone where you are."

Fr. Thom replied, "Cindy, my dear child, I do not know what you are talking about. Whenever Jerome returns, I will try to ask him what is going on. I do wish to assure you that I had nothing to do with anyone coming to your hometown or to your residence." The fact that Fr. Thom said residence rather than job, convinced her that he was unaware of what was going on. Cindy was somewhat satisfied that the old man had nothing to do with his son's visit.

Ray dragged himself around the apartment at a snail pace, literally. It took him an hour to go from living room to the kitchen, along the way knocking over furniture that stood in his way. From time to time, Ray felt like he would pass out. The phone rang again and this time all Ray could manage was to hit the receiver off its cradle. Ray woke up three days later in the hospital. He was at first confused but then remembered those two monsters he had met earlier. Ray thought that if one could compare people to old cars, then the two thugs would come from the worst part of the junk yard. The one with the scar from forehead to chin could be described as the ugliest creature on planet earth, about six feet four inches, three hundred and fifty pounds or otherwise the one with the strong odor of alcohol mixed with garlic on his breath. In Ray's estimation, he could play the part of King Kong, without any make-up. On the other hand, Marble Eye could be described as Mr. Cool or Mr. Smooth, he was well-dressed, well-groomed, gentleman like, but far removed from being a gentleman. He stood approximately six feet eight inches, weighing more than three hundred pounds. They could both be in the heavyweight division, or even Suma Wrestlers. If Ray had to choose, his choice would be Marble Eye because without a doubt he seemed to be super cool, yet in hindsight, Mr. Super Cool turned out to be one of the meanest men on the planet.

Ray ached all over and it was extremely painful to be

alive. He had numerous cracked ribs. He had a concussion. His body and head ached. He was lucky to be alive.

Jerome had felt that something was wrong and had contacted New York's finest, the NYPD, by phone to find out if Ray was okay. That call saved Ray's life. The cops found Ray unconscious and summoned EMS. Had Ray stayed in his apartment without medical attention for another two hours, he would be dead. After Ray regained full consciousness and his general condition had improved, two detectives tried in vain to find out from him who had done this to him.

But he thought it best not to have the cops involved. Ray was tempted to file a police report but thought better than to jeopardize this situation. Those thugs would spare nothing to come after him a second time. He made remarkable recovery but when the time came for his discharge, he was reluctant to leave, for fear of those two thugs. His main goal was to make it back to Massachusetts or find himself a permanent disguise. He would very much prefer if he were in Jerome's position, right now, rather than the precarious situation he had placed himself in. While in the hospital, Ray was sharing a room with a prisoner and there was a cop on duty twenty-four hours per day for the three weeks he was hospitalized. He knew he was pretty safe until his discharge, which was fast approaching.

He felt weak and was hoping he would have some more time to get stronger and at least hatch out a plan to stay out of sight and away from those goons. Ray really didn't have a solution to his problem. His friend John had brought him fresh clothes. He knew that he could spend a few days at John's house but he was afraid he might lead those goons to John. John had also accumulated five thousand dollars during Ray's absence, from outstanding monies Ray's customers owed him.

There was a lot more money out in the streets to be collected. But Ray was sure that the interest on what he owed would have accumulated to more than ten thousand, perhaps fifteen or twenty grand. Once again, Ray decided he did not want to find out. He wanted badly not to be seen leaving the hospital.

CHAPTER SIX

Finally, the dreaded day came. Ray was discharged with a follow-up appointment scheduled for a week later. He still had some issues with his hearing, and from time to time double vision. His attending physician told him that he might have some neurological damage, so he would need to see a neurologist for evaluation and treatment within the next thirty days. When he got all his discharge papers, Ray did not leave the hospital immediately, instead he headed straight to the emergency room. His only thought was if he might befriend a paramedic and see if the paramedic would agree to take him to John's apartment by ambulance.

Crew after crew refused to oblige Ray's unusual request but then a paramedic jokingly said to Ray, "why not try the morgue guy, they might be willing to help." Bells went off in Ray's head. He decided he had nothing to lose, why not give it a shot. Ray was becoming desperate. He knew that if word got out on the street of his discharge, then he would be in danger. He was also sure that he did not want to go up against those miniature sumo wrestlers in good health. Ray was simply too weak to fight. Ray had discussed his transfer home via ambulance with his social worker who told him, that was an unusual request, since he was back on his feet and able to walk. Usually ambulance transfers to home were done for elderly patients with severe respiratory, heart problems and those who are unable to walk. "Try the morgue guy" those words kept going through his head. Ray was desperate and he had nothing to lose. It seemed a good option if he could put a twist to it. It also seemed like the only good option considering the fact that the paramedics were not really going to help.

So he followed directions to the morgue and struck up a conversation with the morgue technician. He told the technician he had a bet with his friend that he was not afraid to ride in a hearse with human remains. Ray was lucky, there was a scheduled pickup in twenty minutes or less. He made the driver of the funeral home an offer he could not refuse. He flashed him a couple hundred dollars. The funeral home driver was more than happy to oblige. He made it safely to John's house in his hearse, the driver told him he would be delighted to repeat the favor any time he had another bet. It was 2:00 am when Ray got to John's apartment where to lie low for a few more weeks.

The relationship between Jerome and his father these days was not on the best of terms since Fr. Thom's last conversation with Cindy and once again Jerome's disappearance for another week. Jerome kept more and more to himself. He seemed to have lost focus and definitely displayed signs of agitation, anger, resentment and aggression towards his father.

The Deadly Priest

Fr. Thom was having a hard time dealing with Jerome's problem. He had decided to transfer Jerome out of his Diocese as a last effort to save his health. Jerome would leave for Detroit, Michigan in four to six weeks. He was not at the Diocese much these days, making frequent trips to New York, or so the old man thought.

Jerome felt comfortable and confident that he held the key to fixing the problem with Cindy. He knew he was close. Finding her home address and work place was ingenious. He convinced himself that he could be whatever he wanted to be, a PI, maybe a lawyer or perhaps a doctor. He convinced himself that he was intelligent and intellectual enough to play any role he chose. His disguise as Hector went well. He was Jerome PI.

On the other hand, he was enraged that his Father had even entertained the thought to have him transferred. He felt that the aging priest was not capable of keeping the blackmailer in check. What if, while he was in Michigan, his Father died? Cindy might panic and report the matter to the cops. She was paid handsomely from the church. I do regret what I did. At that time I was fresh from a crazy trip to New York with that wayward brother of mine. Jerome was good at convincing anyone, especially himself, that his thoughts were correct. He convinced himself that Cindy was scared to go to the authorities. But he felt more and more that his Father was incapable of handling the situation. He resolved that he would take charge of this situation, once and for all. Jerome told his father flatly, "Dad, in the future I will be handling all calls from Cindy." His father disagreed.

And all hell broke loose.

Jerome flew into a rage. He was like a crazed boxer in the ring and he now forgot his game plan. He forgot all that his trainer told him in between rounds. Jerome forgot all about his father's Psychiatric evaluation pending and went off on his father.

He ranted "Dad, for thirty-six years I stood by and saw you dominate my mother, my brother, myself and four sisters. It was always your way. I have seen you hit my mother on more than one occasion. I tried to be the good child you wanted me to be out of fear but as the years went by my fear grew into hate. I couldn't wait until I grew up so you could no longer hurt me. My hurt grew into hate and I must let you know that I feel that the great career goal you chose for me is the very reason that we sit here right now arguing who should speak to Cindy. Thanks to you, both of you have ruined my life, you and Cindy. You made me to be what you could not be."

"You expected me, a young man, to live a straight and upright life, without a woman and without sex." You had women and concubines with your wife. You were sometimes a devil to my mother. Then when you thought you did enough, you ran back to the church to pick-up where you left off. You presented yourself as a dedicated, devout, sacred priest to those who didn't know you that well. I have heard rumors about Cindy. I wish I knew if they were true. The more I think about it, the more things are beginning to make sense to me. The more I think the clearer the pieces seem to fit. I understand the reason why Olga was paid that settlement. So she could move to another state.

"It was a well orchestrated plan. The settlement was not about me and Cindy, it was about you and Olga and that is why Cindy hardly got any of the money and that is why Cindy does not know where her mother is. The plan was to make me the fall Guy, make it seem that I had sex with a minor. Olga could be paid legally by the church to move on with a promise never to expose the real truth. The real truth being that Fr. Thom is the biological father of Cindy. So I was right in thinking that it was inconceivable that a fifteen year old would hatch out a plan of this nature.

"You two have sold your children's legal birth rights for your own indiscretion, Olga for money and you for continued power and position. Your plan was so well orchestrated and executed that, even now, Cindy does not know what really hit her. All she can think of doing is trying to collect money. Poor child, she has not a clue that we were set up. No doubt her mother made her believe that I was the greatest person on earth."

"The plot and settlement was not due to Jerome and Cindy, but it had to do with Olga and Thomas, never to expose this devout head of the Diocese, as you would like people to think you are. The more I think, the more I see the reason why you don't want me to speak to Cindy and it is even more the reason for me to find Olga. So she can shed light on your extracurricular activities. The more I think of this situation, the more I can see just why you are so protective of Cindy. The more I think about it, the more I come to realize that if Olga is not alive, she disappeared or died under mysterious circumstances. It is all coming to me now, Father. I am hoping what I am feeling is not the truth. I am hoping, for your sake, that this is a bad dream, because the pieces sure fit together. It is beginning to look too much like a murder mystery unfolding. So here again, to clear your name from everything, you sent Olga, Nathaniel and Cindy away. So now the next step is to send Jerome away to remove any threat.

"At first, when I didn't give it a lot of thought it seemed farfetched that a fifteen year old would hatch such a plan of blackmail. The more I add up the pieces, the more I seem to understand that this was not Cindy's plan, but the plan of an adult or adults carried out by a minor."

The monologue continued, "Olga's motive more than likely was to keep the truth from her husband. Olga was a crack addict, so too her husband, and it's a small wonder that at times, some addicts would prostitute their children, if they had to in order to pay for their habit. Right now, it is all coming together, and I am hoping to God that I am wrong. But what other motive can there be?

"This may very well be the reason why Olga is nowhere close to Cindy, even though they probably live less than ten miles apart. Dad, I must let you know the whereabouts of Olga is unknown but I am sure this is not news to you."

Jerome was not supposed to let his father know that he knew about Olga, but Jerome forgot his game plan completely. "From what I was made to understand, they live near each other but are not in touch." The pieces were beginning to fit for Fr. Thom as well.

Based on Cindy's recent phone call, he was now convinced that Jerome was snooping around conducting his own investigation.

Jerome went on. "Father, if she is not alive, what did you do with the body? Did you kill her or have her killed? I know you will stop at nothing to stop her blackmailing you. What did she do? Come calling again for more money? I guess now in hindsight you realize your biggest mistake was to settle with a crack addict. Father, even though I may seem to be in trouble, it seems to me that my situation is just the tip of the iceberg. Father, I am sure before you die, I will squeeze that truth out of you."

Fr. Thom was not aware that Jerome had seen Cindy face to face or that his reason for contacting Cindy was because there was absolutely no trace of Olga her mother. Among other things, Jerome now longed to find Olga, even more at this point in the game. Jerome suddenly realized this whole thing could be a set-up. Jerome continued his tirade. "There is a lot that you need to let me know or I may be the one exposing you to the Diocese."

"What did you do? Separate Olga from her child, in order to keep your situation a secret. Or did you have her killed? Despite all you have done, you still had the nerve to try to turn the tables on me, like I am the monster. When you know full well that you and she hatched this plan to save both your skins.

"Nathaniel, Olga's husband had to be a fool not to get a DNA test. Even though once the money kept coming, he didn't give a damn if Thanksgiving fell on a Sunday. You both knew this and that is how you exploited the situation. You have exploited everyone and now you are down to the final two, the key players in your conspiracy. Father, despite your failing health and lying on your death bed, you would like to put the final nail in my coffin. You would like to make me feel guilty, like I did something so horrible, that you can walk away from your wrong-doings at my expense. Are you my father or my enemy? Father, you are old, you should keep that final nail for your own coffin.

"Making me feel guilty for what I did, if you were man enough, I would have known whether Cindy was my sister or not before all this came about.

"Had you stood up as a man and accepted your responsibility in the first place this would not even be happening.

"My Father, I am left to wonder are you a priest, a con artist or a gangster? Let alone the head of the Diocese.

"Repent and confess and God will forgive you. He will take care of you. I know right now I will not forgive you until I can put an end to this mess. Father, you know your son is smart, but how long did you think you could keep me in this Diocese and keep the truth from me?"

Fr. Thom just muttered a few inaudible senile words but he was at the point of being enraged. However, he wanted to appear like he was taking it cool. On the other hand, Jerome could not contain his anger. He could not stop himself from lashing out at his father with the hope he could receive a confession to what now appeared to be the truth. Jerome continued to pile on his wrath despite Fr. Thom's apparent lack of comprehension. It was like someone trying to talk sense to a drunk or speaking to a deaf person, yet Jerome was worked up and could not stop. Now he had to let it all out.

"I am now convinced that I have not done half as bad as you did and, for all I now know, you may be in deeper trouble than I am right now. Let me assure you, from what I can see even though I have no proof, this situation is bigger and more complex than it appears to be. Give it a closer look and I am just amazed at your part in this plot. Let me assure you, I have not covered half of what I think you have done with this conversation or discussion if you want to call it that."

Jerome would not stop digging for the answers and he felt he was on the right track. "Then after all is said and done you turn around and come to the church for atonement and forgiveness and say Lord!! Lord!! And expect to be forgiven.

"Maybe God can forgive you but I am sorry, I have traded forgiveness for hate. I haven't the slightest sliver of love for you, especially for the way you treated my mother before her final demise, her death. Then, as if that is not enough, now you choose to set me up for your personal gains. I have had enough of your dominating behavior and attitude. I refuse to be treated like your nine year old child. Speaking about children, where are your children now? The greatest father in the world, a church-priest, why aren't your children here in your time of need in your final days?

"The evil that men do lives on after them. None of your children can stand you and when you have passed on I am sure none of them will shed a tear.

Screaming and in tears. Jerome said "may God have mercy on your soul."

Fr. Thom was speechless for a while. When he finally recovered fully and could muster a few words, he made it clear to Jerome that he would have no more of Jerome's outbursts because he would be the one to go to the authorities rather than Cindy.

Jerome told his father "I may be doing that before you do, because of what I know now I am sure you cannot afford an investigation."

Jerome's response was out of anger, but he felt he now had the upper hand with this situation. The only way he could stay ahead was to let his father know what he suspected. Jerome thought he was close to the truth and he only needed a confession or proof.

Jerome almost knocked his father over on the way out. It seemed like he was temporarily insane. He had lost it. He had forgotten that he was a priest. It seemed now that he could care less what happened to his father. In Jerome's mind a heart attack would help his cause more than hurt it. A heart attack could be the easy way out since his father had a history.

As for his mental condition, Fr. Jerome only hoped his Father would remember this day for a very long time. Jerome saw his father as a threat. He thought more and more of a way to get rid of this obstacle that was standing in his way. It became clear to Jerome that his father was protecting Cindy and trying to keep her and Jerome apart, lest they should compare notes and find out the truth. Cindy already knew about Fr. Thom being her father. Yet there was no certainty. It seemed to be Olga's way to get control over Thomas. The possibility only existed, or so she led Fr. Thom to believe. Fr. Thom was not about to find out. He was too deeply preoccupied with the problems at hand. He was concerned that he was losing his grip on Jerome, and then he had the problem if Cindy found out the truth of her paternity. Fr. Thom was not going to dare Olga and her threat to find out the truth and risk her exposing his wrong doing to the church, even though she was not around these days. His biggest mistake was to mess with a crack addict.

The big question Jerome was hoping to have answered from his father was Olga's whereabouts. Was she living or was she dead? With either outcome Jerome thought now he was in the driver's seat. His detective work had paid off.

Jerome thought about Ray for a moment and wondered how he was doing. He figured he knew where he could find his brother. The following day he left the Diocese but this time no one knew where he was headed. What would it be this time New York City, Albany or someplace else?

Jerome met with Ray in New York City and they hatched out a plan that Jerome would assist Ray to leave John's apartment, disguised as a priest. By this time Jerome was becoming an expert at disguises, or so he thought. This time he could be the priest he was, he would play himself and help Ray with his disguise. This was fun for Jerome, maybe due to lack of excitement. His life had been void of excitement until Cindy came calling the Diocese. Jerome liked the little intrigue for the moment. No one would be watching them, or at least so they thought. The plan worked and the two priests left John's apartment bound for Albany with the plan for Ray to obtain a new identity and together they could work to take care of Cindy and put an end to the threat.

Fr. Jerome really had great hopes that his brother would be his savior. He had in the back of his mind "murder for hire." Jerome was waiting for the right opportunity to present his idea to his brother. Ray was not even considered a small time thug. His thing was pimps, prostitutes, sale of drugs and gambling. Murder for hire was not Ray's modus operandi. He was not an angel. He did have an arrest record for minor offenses like propositioning a prostitute, possession of marijuana, public drunkenness, shoplifting and other minor offenses. But Ray was spared jail time and was really not ready for the big time. Occasionally, he did a little bouncer gig at his friend's bar. He was not ready for the big house and he sure was not ready for Jerome's plan of murder. Ray was not even thinking along the lines his brother was planning.

CHAPTER SEVEN

THREE WEEKS LATER

With Jerome's whereabouts unknown, the old priest disappeared without a trace. The news of the sudden disappearance of Fr. Thom hit every newsstand in Massachusetts. It was a sensational news story. It wasn't everyday that a priest disappears, let alone the head of the Diocese. As a matter of fact, Fr. Thom was the only priest in the Catholic Church's history to disappear without a trace.

Fr. Jerome had left with little fanfare. With father and son gone at the same time, this led to a lot of speculations. Although it was well known by insiders about Jerome's impending transfer, his whereabouts still remained a speculation. The Diocese kept Jerome's absence a secret, treating the matter as though he had left on vacation prior to his father's disappearance. Some of the members however, thought it odd because of the strained relationship between father and son, which by this time was apparent to most insiders.

The FBI was looking at the old priest's disappearance with suspicion and Jerome was considered a person of interest. In the beginning, the Diocese decided against telling the investigating officers about Jerome but as questions were asked, the truth came to light.

Twenty-four hours went by and the old priest did not show up. The following day, the police and prominent members of the clergy and business owners organized a massive search for Fr. Thom. The search went on for over sixteen hours, but no one seemed to be able to shed light on the disappearance of the old priest

Once the media got word that Jerome had gone on vacation just prior to his father's disappearance, the news media painted a sensational picture of Jerome being a suspect. One headline read "Head of Diocese Disappears after Announcing Son's Transfer." Speculation ran high. Another headline read "Father and Son Elope."

The Diocese released information that Jerome was on vacation to keep things quiet and play down the media hype. Jerome learned about his assumed vacation on the news. He was happy that this news release would enhance his position. He knew he would need to establish an airtight alibi, due to the future plans he had for his father. Jerome was not on vacation, he was AWOL.

Three days into the search, Jerome showed up, and the attention of all was on him. The media, members of the clergy, the local police and FBI were all interested to hear where he was, the biggest question was where had he been the night Fr. Thom disappeared.

At first the questioning from Detective Lieutenant Collins from the Homicide/Special Victims Squad and Special Agent Baines seemed routine but as time went by the questioning grew more and more intense.

Jerome's alibi was that he had spent time in Albany, New York with a female friend named Kelly. It took their counterparts in New York three to four days to locate Kelly. It was actually the news media that found out that Kelly was a prostitute and that bit of information directed the cops where to search for her. Had Fr. Thom not disappeared, this piece of news would have been sensational. A priest shacking up with a prostitute for a number of days was news, but their focus was on the investigation of the disappearance of Fr. Thom. Jerome did receive some heat from the clergy but all eyes and ears were focused on information of his father. More and more, no one trusted Fr. Jerome in this situation.

His information checked out eventually, but he did not mention his trip to New York. Investigators asked him if he would be willing to take a lie detector test but he was reluctant. Imagine a priest unwilling to take a lie detector test. Jerome's action aroused more suspicion but at the moment the police did not have a body, so even though the attention was on Jerome the police did not have enough to charge him with a crime.

Lieutenant Collins decided to follow up closely with what the prostitute had to say, since it was the only thing he had to go on. Therefore he decided to travel to Albany, accompanied by Special Agent Baines to interview the prostitute. It took the two Detectives the better part of a week to locate Kelly. She was holed up in a motel, being supplied all her needs by Ray so she did not have to work regularly, and more so because Fr. Jerome did not want her on the streets with the information she now had.

Once the two priests arrived safely in Albany, Ray and Jerome separated. They did not see each other for two weeks; that was part of Jerome's ingenious plan. That accounted for the two weeks total he was away from the Diocese. Stopping in only briefly to be seen at the Diocese, long enough to tell his father off. Jerome was indeed brilliant. First he stayed with Kelly for a few days after his visit to Cindy to establish an alibi. Then after going back to the Diocese for a few days he left to assist Ray with his disguise and move to Albany. He then convinced Ray that it would be better if they were not seen together in Albany. Giving himself time to kidnap his father, Ray thought that the situation was a little odd, but went along with his brother's request, none the less. Ray's thoughts were that Jerome might be afraid the thugs got word of their whereabouts and find him instead of Ray. He had no idea what his brother's plans were. Jerome was a lot more desperate than Ray could imagine. Ray was not aware that in a few days after arriving from New York City, he would come once again face to face with his father.

THE MEETING

Fr. Jerome thought it best not to tell his brother what he was planning until the time came. Or that he had already put the first part of his plan in place. So, it came as a total surprise when Jerome invited Ray to his motel even though he had suggested that they should stay apart from each other. Ray was dumbfounded when he showed up at Jerome's motel to find his father there. He was at a loss for words. Even though happy to see both his brother and father together again, Ray was in total shock wondering what his brother was planning for the old man.

He tried to have good positive thoughts about what was going down, but he could only come up with negative thoughts based on his brother's hate filled comments about his father in recent times. Jerome was able to convince his father that Ray was in some trouble and desperately needed to be with him through his crisis.

Fr. Thom was suddenly confused and scared at the same time and now realized that he could be in danger. The pieces were suddenly beginning to fit. He now realized that his son, or sons, would stop at nothing to get him out of the way. That explained why Jerome had convinced him just before leaving the Diocese not to tell anyone he was leaving. Jerome told his father "you will only be gone for two hours." That was two days ago. It suddenly occurred to the senior priest that this could very well be the reason that he was sleeping so much, the past few days. Fr. Thom now knew his son had drugged him.

The secretive way Jerome had whisked him away from the Diocese in the middle of the night was no longer a mystery to Fr. Thom. The female costume Jerome wore now explained a lot, Jerome did not want anyone to know he was at the Diocese the night Fr. Thom disappeared. There was a lot that didn't make sense at the time that was now making sense to the old priest.

Jerome broke the silence and the old priest's train of thought. He began addressing Ray and his father.

"I know this has come as a surprise to both of you seeing each other is a bittersweet situation, but I had to summon this unexpected meeting. This important meeting has been brought about because of a crisis in both of our lives. Ray, I did tell Dad half of the truth to get him here mysteriously, the other part I did not tell. Now Dad, you have that confused look on your face so let me deal with you first. I am not going to prison because of Cindy and I refuse to be blackmailed by her. Ray has agreed to help me take care of that problem. In exchange I will help Ray take care of his problem so that he can resume his normal life style.

"In the meantime, Father you will be under his care with the understanding that you will not answer the telephone or read any newspaper. Ray will take good care of you in my absence. I will return to Massachusetts so that everything will look normal. Ray, you are left with a choice of kidnapping or an accessory to kidnapping. If we all cooperate, I guarantee we will all be fine. As the robbers say, cooperate and no one will get hurt. Ray, as part of our agreement, you will keep that prostitute away from the Police and FBI."

Now that Jerome had laid the groundwork of his plot, he felt powerful. He knew that Ray had no choice in the matter but to go along with him because he held the solution to Ray's new identity.

Jerome, from school days, remained in contact with a

classmate, now living in Ohio, who could make any fake identification look real, an ace computer hacker who could reproduce any document with corresponding matching serial numbers. This makes the document authentic even when scanned by a computer.

Mitch, Jerome and Ray went to school together, but right after leaving high school, Mitch's family moved to Cleveland. Jerome stayed in touch with Mitch. Ray did not. Mitch did time for identity theft. While in prison the warden did not allow Mitch anywhere near a copier or computer because Mitch once made himself a release document signed by the warden and almost got out. The Warden could not tell the difference in the two signatures. All he knew was that he did not sign Mitch's release documents. The signature Mitch produced was a perfect, identical match of the warden's.

Mitch earned himself another eighteen months added onto his time for forgery but at the same time earned the respect of the warden. Mitch said it was the best he could do with the limited resources within his reach. After all, he was in prison. He was not at home in his lab.

During the two weeks Ray spent by himself, he staked out Cindy's job gathering information for Jerome but making sure to keep out of Cindy's sight. Keeping his father also in his sight He hit a few nightclubs and bars. Along the way he met an ex-con named Jimmy. Ray and Jimmy hit it off the first night they met and ever since they met Ray began spending more and more time at Jimmy's home when Jimmy was not out clubbing.

Jerome was bent on taking out Cindy. It seemed like the only answer to his problem. There are only two solutions to blackmail; either move to a foreign country or remove the blackmailer. The third remote solution is to come forward and own up to the blackmail information. Once the information is revealed the blackmail is over. However, Jerome knew he could not use option three. Had it not been for his father's greed for power and position, his father could possibly use option three in the beginning, Now it may be a little too late. Jerome did not tell Ray what he had in mind.

But now, Ray sensed what was coming down. For the first time, Ray gave serious thought to Jerome and his problem and came face to face with the ramifications involved.

Ray underestimated his brother due to his PAPAL responsibilities. Ray didn't consider his brother a killer. Let alone a double murderer. But from recent developments, Ray now realized the possibility for a double murder was evolving. His father and Cindy must have a lot to be concerned about. Ray hoped that his train of thought was incorrect for the sake of all involved. His father, and Jerome, in particular. This was one puzzle Ray was not in a position to figure out. One thing Ray was sure about, he did not want to see harm come to his father at any cost.

Jerome's resolve was to get rid of Cindy. Ray on the other hand was not going to be a contract killer. Ray preferred not to be involved with this whole charade.

Ray did not see murder as a solution. Jerome, on the

other hand, probably based his decision on the scripture that says "if your right hand is causing you to stumble, cut it off." Cindy was indeed Jerome's right hand in this situation.

Jerome, a priest and a brilliant scholar, he of all people should know that this passage of scripture was used figuratively. Now, for his convenience, it was being used literally.

The more Lieutenant Collins and his partner, Special Agent Baines, questioned Kelly, the more convinced they were that Kelly was not speaking the truth. When the detectives first located Kelly, they showed her a photo of Jerome. She said they had spent approximately two weeks in a motel but she did not tell them that they were joined by his brother and an elderly man a week later. Kelly was paid handsomely to lie about the two weeks stay, when in fact, Jerome was only there with her for three days at the most.

When shown a picture of his father and asked if she had seen him she lied. She also did not mention to the police that Jerome had told her that the old man had come to Albany for a surgical procedure. Jerome never told Kelly that Father Thom was his biological father. The cops knew that she was not telling them all that she knew.

Kelly was now the key to their investigation, if only she would tell the lieutenant the truth. However, she was paid handsomely to lie, and Ray kept her with an adequate supply of drugs. Kelly hated cops and was not about to tell the lieutenant the truth.

Kelly was like an animal that had to hunt for its own food. Now, suddenly being placed in captivity and no longer having to hunt for her supply of drugs, at this stage, she would not do anything to jeopardize her regular supply of drugs.

The two Detectives decided to stick around for a few days. Since they had no other information, they would follow Kelly around to see where she went and who she spoke with. They were interested to know who this James person was and to ask him a few questions about the priest. As soon as the detectives left, Kelly was on the phone to Ray, who she came to know as James. Kelly was beginning to fall in love with Ray.

She first met Jerome but really cared for Ray because of his apparent bad boy image. He seemed aggressive like her previous pimp. Kelly was used to having a pimp and her last pimp had died a few months before from a gunshot wound. The killer was never caught. She lied for Jerome, only because Ray told her to do so. Now, she realized that Ray or Jerome was in some kind of trouble and Ray had not told her that the old man was in some way related to the two brothers.

Kelly soon figured out that the ailing man they referred to as George, could be the missing priest from Massachusetts.

The photograph on television bore a striking resemblance to the old man, although Ray and Jerome never let her get a really good look at him. But something about this whole affair seemed to her a little fishy now that detectives were questioning her.

Ray told her not to try to contact him at the motel,

but he said he would be in touch with her the following day. He had paid for her room for two days in advance knowing that he would not return, giving himself two days to play with.

Ray stayed one step ahead of the police He now moved his father into his new friend's home in the suburbs. It was never his idea to participate in Jerome's plans, especially against his father, even though he harbored similar feelings towards his father as Jerome did. Ray was an advocate of the life in prison rather than the death penalty type. Therefore, he preferred to let his father live as long as possible to suffer for all that he did in the past, rather than to kill him and take him out of his misery.

Ray knew that Jimmy could be trusted because he had a long rap sheet dating back to nineteen sixty nine for armed robbery, kidnapping, and rape, and once he was found not guilty for murder due to insufficient evidence. Ray knew that ex-cons were not rats, so he felt safe staying at Jimmy's home.

Jimmy had not been in any kind of trouble for the last five years and he was working for an armored car company. He had lied on his application and got the job because he was fresh out of California. A criminal background check was done. But at the time of his hire, fingerprinting was really not a requirement. Jimmy held on to that job because he was planning the heist of his own truck, but could not find anyone willing to participate. Ray seemed interested or could supply the manpower Jimmy needed for the job. In exchange for Ray's favor, Jimmy would kill Cindy.

Meanwhile, Fr. Thom's health was deteriorating. He

The Deadly Priest

was made to exist on one week supply of medication over the past three weeks. He was very weak and could hardly walk.

Lieutenant Collins followed Kelly to a Motel 16. Ray had already left, but he did not checkout. Kelly still had keys to the room because she was used to picking up her daily supply of drugs which she got on this trip to the motel. She knew where Ray left her supply. After Kelly left, the two detectives, on a hunch questioned the motel clerk. They got the lucky break they were looking for.

They found out that a week before, the prostitute and three men shared the two adjoining rooms. One of the rooms that Kelly had just left was still occupied by the one known as James, since he had not yet checked out. Check out time would be eleven the following day. The clerk described two of the men, one description fit Jerome, and then the clerk indicated that the third man appeared to be in his late seventies, he appeared to be pale and weak. James, the one that still remained sad that the old man would be going for heart surgery in a few days.

The cops asked the clerk when did he leave? The clerk could not say when. The cops asked the clerks permission to look around the rooms. He obliged and the cops looked around both rooms.

The now vacant room was already cleaned however; they still found enough evidence, for a joint venture investigation involving themselves and Albany forensic department. Inspector Collins summoned the

FBI, and decided to wait for James to return to the motel.

Kelly was picked up on prostitution charges, to prevent her from returning to what was now a crime scene. The hotel management was contacted and told not to rent either of the two rooms, until the investigation was completed.

With the FBI now on the case, the two detectives returned to Massachusetts to continue to question Jerome, now convinced that he knew something about the disappearance of his father.

Jerome continued to deny having anything to do with his father's disappearance and without a body, there was very little the cops could do. They asked Jerome if he knew a guy named James. He said he did not know James, although he knew it was Ray they were asking about. Jerome also denied staying at that motel, because he knew that they would try to link Ray to him.

Jerome said he just spent a few hours at the motel with a prostitute and did not remember its name though it could be Motel 16. Jerome insisted he spent most of his time at a friend's house but did not want to disclose the name of that person he stayed at because she was married and her husband was a Marine away on duty in Iraq.

Jerome went back and forth with his story. The longer each interview went, the more convinced the Detectives were that Jerome was their prime suspect. He was not a good liar. They now had enough to get a search warrant and a wire tap. They decided against arresting Jerome, but instead kept him under twenty four hour surveillance to see who he spoke to and where he went.

CSI, on instruction from the FBI, dusted the two rooms and they lifted fingerprints of Jerome, Kelly and two sets of unknown prints. They could not be sure who those prints belonged to. Perhaps a previous guest maybe. In order to verify the old priest's prints they would still have to locate him because there was no match for him on file.

Fingerprints usually place a person at the scene. Date and time cannot be determined from fingerprints. But should those unknown prints belong to the old man, then the situation would be interesting, since Jerome admits being in that motel and his prints are there as proof he was there. Even though there is still nothing to verify the exact time a print is made, it would be a big coincidence that the older priests fingerprints were found there at that same motel where Jerome admits to staying, even if he was there for an hour. If either of the unknown prints could be matched to his father, then one thing would be certain. Jerome shared the same space his father did at sometime. Once his father's fingerprints could be identified at that motel, then Fr. Jerome would have a lot of explaining to do.

Kelly had no idea at the time what was going on. She had only caught a glimpse of the old man. Honestly she was not aware that, first he was kidnapped and secondly, he was a priest.

While in custody she was grilled over and over about these three men. She did identify Jerome from photographs even though he disguised himself with a long beard. She maintained that the other two men, James and the old man joined them briefly at the motel and stayed there for a few hours at the most. She said she was pretty sure Jerome did not leave the motel for longer than two hours on any given day, but confirmed Jerome spent a few days, not hours, at the motel with her. Kelly also told the cops she did not have to work so she stayed with Jerome for most of the time. He rarely left the motel. Kelly explained that most of the time Jerome gave her money to take care of her drug habit. She continued to lie, the more they questioned her. The more she lied and the deeper she was getting herself in as an accessory to kidnapping.

The cops knew that she was lying. When Kelly was arrested, she had in her possession two twenty dollar bags of heroine. The detectives promised to prosecute her only for prostitution in exchange for information pertaining to this kidnapping case. Then, they began threatening her, saying that they would definitely prosecute her for the heroine possession since in their estimation she was not telling the truth. Kelly continued to be defiant. Where was James? By what method did she contact him?

She told the cops they were both casual acquaintances and she did not do a background check on the men. The cops knew that she was lying but somehow they believed the part that she did not know a whole lot about the men. Most prostitutes do not make it a point to find out about their Johns. All they need to know is that he can pay for her trick.

"Kelly, do you realize that you were involved with

kidnapping and if you do not come clean with us you will be charged as an accessory to kid-napping, which carries a maximum sentence of twenty years?" Asked one of the cops.

"Well" said Kelly "I did not kidnap anyone. I was only hanging out with two guys and an old man. They did not tell me they had kidnapped the old guy. So there is nothing you can pin on me."

Kelly was right and the Detectives knew it, since she was not aware of a kidnapping, the least they could charge her with was obstruction of justice.

"I am not even sure what you are telling me now; that the guy was kidnapped is the truth. That is what you are saying. To be honest I have told you all I know. If you continue to harass me I will ask to see my lawyer." Kelly was growing tired of the questioning. She knew the maximum she could do for the drugs would be twelve to eighteen months and if she could convince these Detectives she was telling the truth they might not even press charges. They were more interested in finding out what happened to the old man.

Meanwhile, word was out that Scar Face and Marble Eye were in Albany looking for Ray. Ray knew he would have to lie low, taking things one day at a time. He knew from past experience that those guys could not be taken lightly, literally speaking. His last encounter was still fresh in his mind. Ray relived his experience of the night he came in contact with the two thugs and, even though the time frame of the torture was less than fifteen minutes all together, thoughts of that night sent a chill down Ray's spine.

Indeed, the thugs were in Albany and they were asking questions about Ray. No one knew Ray by that name they only knew a James that fit that description, but nobody knew his whereabouts except that he stayed at some nearby motel accompanied from time to time by a prostitute.

This information seemed to fit Ray and the duo seemed to think that he was actually using an alias to hide his identity. The thugs had applied pressure to John, Ray's friend who had a slightly similar experience with them as Ray did. John had no other alternative but to give them what information he knew about Ray. The thugs reassured John that if his information proved to be a lie, they would pay him another visit but this time they were sure their second visit, would be fatal.

After their visit to John, he had to undergo surgery to restore the use of his groin area. John had to use a foley catheter for three months after his surgery. John thought that he never wanted to see or hear from Ray again and hoped that Ray was hiding out in Albany so he would not have to see Scar Face and Marble Eye again.

Cindy heard all about what was going on in Lowell. She thought she could provide some of the answers to what was going on but thought that she would prefer to wait things out. However, there was something that bothered her very much. She had recognized the face of Jerome in the newspaper as closely resembling that of Hector, she thought to herself. She was sure that Jerome had to be Hector, but still had some doubts that Jerome would go so far as to come looking for her disguised as a private investigator.

Cindy still had the business card of Hector. Since she had never called the number, she never even thought to look at it, but now she was more than curious to know who this number belonged to. She dialed the number from a pay phone and it was no surprise that the phone number given on the card was a direct line to Jerome at the Diocese. Now everything seemed to make sense to Cindy. The pieces were falling into place.

She was pretty sure that when she first saw Hector, as he called himself, she was looking at the image of Jerome. Though it was a few years ago, both had put on a few pounds. Cindy knew that there could now be no mistake. The so called Hector was indeed Fr. Jerome.

Now she had concrete proof because Jerome was on the other end of the line. Cindy was furious because he had the nerve to track her down in person, and the balls to tell her now that he had information that would benefit her for a fee of twenty-five hundred dollars.

No wonder the old priest had disappeared. He had disappeared at the hands of his son now. I wonder what next he is planning. Could it be that I am next, she wondered.

CHAPTER EIGHT

Cindy could not contain her anger; her first response to him was "what would you prefer to be called, Hector or Fr. Jerome?"

He knew it had to be Cindy. So he ignored her question and went on straight to the business at hand. He was longing for this moment, yet he knew he had to be cautious with what he said and how he said it.

In a calm voice Jerome said, "Cindy, I was expecting your call but I was hoping that you'd called sooner, you must be careful with what you say on the telephone because the phones here are most likely tapped. That is the reason I was hoping to hear from you sooner. However, if you are ready for the information I told you about, I will be more than happy to meet you where we last met to tell you what you want to know."

Jerome did not think he had to disguise himself any longer. He was sure Cindy knew it was him, disguise or not, he knew once she agreed to meet him he would put an end to the charade.

He felt confident, now that the old man was out of the picture, that he would be able to take care of his own business the way he saw fit. A lot was riding on this

The Deadly Priest

conversation. Maybe even his father's future. Jerome now felt confident, in control and in the driver's seat.

He felt confident that Cindy would fall for the bait, money or not. Now that he knew he had her attention, he would not let her go. He would make her want to call again. Jerome wanted her on his leash.

"The important information I had for you is about Olga." He continued, Cindy froze, for about thirty seconds she did not respond. Olga was Cindy's Mother; she had not seen her for nearly two years. Crack addict or not, she was still her mother.

"Are you still there?" Jerome asked, but there was no answer. Then Jerome heard the dial tone. Cindy was gone but Jerome knew that she would call back.

Jerome did not know anymore about Olga than Cindy, but his calculation at the time they met was for her to call him. He could continue to formulate his deadly plan. He needed motivation to justify his action, however, after this phone call Jerome was not too sure he wanted anything to happen to Cindy, at least not now with all the attention centered on his father's disappearance. Jerome was not sure if the authorities had tapped the Diocese phones. Since they suspected he had something to do with his father disappearance, Fr. Jerome was not sure if incoming phone calls could be traced.

He sure did not want the cops to find out about Cindy. Maybe now he should have listened to his father in the first place, and let him handle Cindy. Then he would not have thoughts of making his father disappear. For the first time, Jerome started to question kidnapping his father. His action has brought a lot of attention to himself and the Diocese. Now he had to be extremely careful.

The only feelings he had for Cindy were of hate and anger, if hate and anger could be described as feelings.

It took Cindy five days before she could muster enough courage to call Jerome again; her curiosity caused her to spend a few sleepless nights in thoughts of her mother. Almost immediately Jerome went to work telling Cindy he could meet with her in one week since he had to meet with a parishioner in her district the following Wednesday. Jerome wanted his conversation with Cindy to appear to be a normal counseling encounter between priest and parishioner. He made his tone normal and almost casual.

Jerome lied. He really did not have a plan in hand and for the first time he wanted Cindy to say no. He knew he could stall her if she did not have the money for the information.

Cindy was once again dumbfounded. She did not have the money nor did she want to meet with Jerome again, for fear that Jerome would do her harm or make her disappear for good, like he did his father. Now Cindy wondered if Jerome or his father had something to do with her mother's disappearance. On the other hand, she could possibly set up Jerome in some way or the other, yet she found it difficult and surprising to admit that after all these years, she still had feelings for him.

Cindy felt pretty sure that Jerome had something to do with the old man's disappearance. This could have a direct bearing on her phone calls to the Diocese. It suddenly occurred to her that the so called Fr. Jerome could be dangerous.

When she last spoke to Fr. Thom, he did make it quite clear to her, she should avoid having any conversations with Jerome. The Senior priest did mention that Jerome was becoming desperate to contact her. With all these unanswered questions plaguing her mind, Cindy's next response would startle Jerome.

"What did you do to your father?" the words came out before Cindy could contain herself. Jerome collected himself, once again reminding himself to be careful what he said. He stalled for time as he struggled to regain his calm demeanor. "I had nothing to do with my father's disappearance; you should refrain from accusing me of something you have no knowledge or proof of. You should know at the time my father disappeared, I was not in the state of Massachusetts. Cindy knew where Jerome was at the time of his father's disappearance but refrained from mentioning anything about her encounter with Hector. Jerome had already confirmed that theory by taking her phone call on Hector's phone number.

Jerome continued, "The FBI did check out my story and verified where I was on the day he disappeared thanks to you. You made it difficult for him and me to get along, because he wanted to do things completely different than what I considered acceptable."

Cindy cut in "I really did not call you for the information you said you had for me. I have no intention of paying you a penny for information other than what happened to your father. He is a kind and just soul and I know whatever I give to you he will refund to me. However, in the meantime I wanted you to know that I am listening out to hear if that poor old priest is not found, because pretty soon you can safely bet your bottom dollar I will go to the police and report your sorry ass." With that Cindy hung up the phone.

This phone call, like the one before, was too short to trace. But these two mysterious phone calls were becoming another loose end or lead that seemed to have a direct bearing on the case. Jerome seemed to have slipped up when he mentioned that because of Cindy he and his father were having difficulty getting along. Even though he wanted Cindy's phone call to sound like a counseling matter, he completely lost his cool and almost blew it.

However, the police still did not think it was time to move in on Jerome as yet. They avoided questioning him about the phone calls. They wanted a clearer understanding of what these two calls were about. The conversation ended too quickly for the call to be traced but law enforcement was now interested in talking to the mysterious caller Cindy about her taped conversation. They only knew her by name but could not piece together her connection to Fr. Jerome or his father. Was this Cindy person a girlfriend or a secret wife or perhaps another prostitute? She was definitely a person of interest.

Cindy had become fond of the old priest and his calm assurance with which he handled things and the money he easily sent her. Now with the old priest out of the way, her money could be in jeopardy because Cindy now knew she could not trust Fr. Jerome. She was now beginning to realize that Jerome was a deadly priest and she hoped that Fr. Thom was okay. On the other hand, she was becoming less and less enthused with Jerome's tactics.

Cindy was in a deep thought about the whole situation when her home phone rang. It was less than thirty minutes since she had spoken to Jerome and she was shocked to find out it was him again on the line calling her from a pay phone.

"Cindy," Jerome blurted out, "I would just like to let you know that I have enough problems on my hands as it is, my father has disappeared and if you think you will go to the cops with any information, of course, it will be speculation. It may compound my situation as a suspect as I am already considered. But on the other hand if you do, I can promise you, you will be sorry. I will not fail to report your little extortion scheme.

"I am willing to work with you to see this thing through, I can also give you the information I have promised you for a fee. Now you can get it for free, but first you will have to promise me you will keep your big mouth shut and stay out of my family affairs."

Jerome was in a compromising situation but at the same time he wanted Cindy to see him as being tough. He wanted her to think that he was not scared of her threat. He wanted her to know he was not like his father. He was not playing with her. Jerome stopped short of telling Cindy if she did not stay out of his business she would get hurt. He was that furious.

Cindy was also furious, how dare him call my

unlisted number, then to insult me. Little does he know I am a member of his family and as such I have every right to be his so called family business.

Cindy exploded "We will both go to prison, I for extortion and you as a sex offender." Cindy was not backing down from Jerome, to her it was a love hate situation outweighed by hate. She shouted. "Jerome, I know extortion is a felony, but which is worse, a devout righteous priest who is also a sex offender? Guess what Fr. Jerome, a felon does not have to register as a felon offender but you will have to register wherever you choose to live as a sex offender. I don't have to tell anyone about you, they will find you out, as a sex offender, kidnapper, and more than likely a double murderer, my mother and more than likely your Father. It is only a matter of time before you are caught because you are not smarter than the law."

They were both speaking at the same time no one caring to hear what the other had to say.

Jerome hit the roof, he went off, not even hearing the line go dead he was in an insane rage, he just had to finish and get his point across. Hello!! Hello as he came to the realization she was gone. He called her again but she did not answer. After several attempts she finally picked up the phone and this time she was listening to what he had to say. Jerome in a calm whisper continued. "Cindy, the disappearance of Fr .Thom has nothing to do with you." He now avoided mention of her mother. "You should have been speaking to me anyway. We are the only two people who knew what happened on that day, it was not all my fault. If you can remember, you always had a crush on me and many times I was the one who avoided you. Then when you turned fifteen, you became bolder. In my moment of weakness I did the unthinkable.

"To my recollection, everything was fine on that occasion because you were not even a virgin. However, on the second occasion we got caught and then it became a problem. You know that the sex was consensual except for the fact that you were a minor under the age of eighteen."

Once again Cindy exploded in response to Jerome's comment on her virginity. She went into a tirade not listening to what he was saying but Cindy made it very clear that she was going to shed light on the investigation as soon as they were off the phone.

Jerome managed to calm Cindy down and continued calmly with his papal monotone.

"I did not say this to my father, because I was too embarrassed to do so, but you know as well as I do, it was not all my doing."

Jerome wanted to tell Cindy what he suspected, now that it seemed he had her undivided attention, but decided to save the best for last. Cindy was quiet on the other end for a while. Jerome said that if she was willing to meet with him he would tell her of the supposed conspiracy theory he was ninety percent sure his father and Olga had executed at their expense.

Cindy's thought went back five years, she knew that what Jerome was saying was the truth, she did in fact have a crush on Jerome and it was her mother who had brought it to Cindy's attention. Her mother told Cindy that Jerome looked at her as a man in love.

At the time, Jerome was young and inexperienced and was scared of being thrown out of the Diocese, after being a priest for only one year. He was more mindful of shame and disgrace, and the fact that he was beginning to like the pace of the parish schedule. He delivered mass two Sundays a month. So at all times he had two weeks to prepare his sermon. The rest of his time was spent answering phones and doing youth counseling, three days a week, five to seven pm. This is when he became even closer to Cindy.

Apart from that, his schedule was far from being hectic, as compared to what he saw when he visited the Big Apple. People, there in New York, as he observed, always seemed to be on the go, running to board trains and buses. It seemed to him as though time went by quicker there. People were always finding it difficult to keep abreast with time.

Jerome resolved that the information he wanted to sell Cindy would be the plot he thought he had uncovered. To keep her quiet, he would even give her the information for free. Finally, Jerome heard the phone go dead, it was obvious she did not put the receiver in the cradle she had just gently pressed down to disconnect the call.

Jerome also reflected on Cindy and once again convinced himself that he was at least able to throw off some of the guilt on her. Judging by her calm, at the end of the phone conversation he thought that he had given her something to think about.

Jerome kept in touch with Ray by phone on a daily basis using pay phones at different locations.

Due to his knowledge of the Diocese grounds, Fr. Jerome would slip out the back unnoticed and disguised as a female, make his daily phone calls to his brother at dusk. Ray told him their father was very ill and would not survive for a long time without immediate medical attention. But they both knew that there was an alert for the old priest, especially at hospitals.

Jerome's calculation now was that his father would die from heart complications rather than at his hands. That way no one will be held directly responsible. In his mind, he was already making preparations to go to Albany to perform his father's last burial rights. Despite all that had transpired in the past, he felt compelled to give his father a decent burial.

However, he was pleased with himself and felt happy how things were turning out. Now he would not have to execute his plan to kill his father, or to have it done by someone.

He said a prayer of thanks that he was spared from committing murder, despite being an accessory in arranging the kidnapping of his father and for being indirectly responsible for his death. In his father's condition, and not being able to take his medication as per his Doctor's orders in itself was a death sentence. Jerome knew that the state of his father's health it would be just a matter of time before the old man succumbed to his eventual death.

Jerome did not think about the consequences of his

actions and that he would be directly responsible for the old man's kidnapping and subsequent death, once there is enough evidence that he played a role in his kidnapping. That was the focus of the investigation and once there was evidence, they would all be charged with second degree murder. Presently, he would be charged with kidnapping, once the authorities could prove he was responsible for the disappearance of his father which carried a penalty of twenty years to life.

Despite being an ex-con, Jimmy disliked the idea of having the priest at his home. Jimmy's focus since reaching Ray was on the heist so he was leery of being caught up in kidnapping. He was becoming impatient to the point of giving Ray and his brother an ultimatum to remove the old man from his home.

The more things developed, the more Ray found himself going deeper into trouble. Ray's thoughts these days were how things would end. Jerome thought he had things figured out. He would let Ray bury his father in the ravine where he stayed, digging his father's grave during the night.

Ray knew he would have to participate in the heist which Jimmy was planning, in order to claim his fair share of the loot. He anticipated it to be more than half a million dollars. His plan would be to take his portion, pay for his new identity and move to any foreign country, perhaps Brazil.

Jimmy had told Ray that on any given day he transported at least three to five million dollars. At first, he wanted no part in the heist, but as time went on, Jimmy made it sound so simple that Ray thought it over and thought about the money. He decided he would go along for the ride but first Scar Face and Marble Eyes had to be taken care of. Jimmy reassured Ray that he could take care of them, once and for all.

Jimmy was a marksman in the service. When he came out of the service he was a member of the elite swat team. Jimmy had won several marksman medals before turning to a life of crime. Jimmy, however, kept his sharp shooting skills honed by hunting on weekends in his spare time. He took Ray on one of his weekend hunting trips and demonstrated his accuracy saying exactly where he would hit his prey.

From their regular conversation, Ray now learned of Jerome's master plan to get rid of his father. Yet, despite his feelings for the way his father had wronged his mother, Ray still did not feel that he should have to answer for his father's death. So he formulated a plan of his own to take care of this situation. He continued to put plans in place for his father's funeral, careful to transport the dirt he dug each night at least one hundred and fifty yards away, and spread it out level in the swamp. This was hard work. Ray also made sure at the end of the day, he covered the make shift grave with camouflage that made the ground look natural. He would wait until it grew dark, then he would make his way through the hedges to Jimmy's house to await his brother's phone call. Each day Ray would bring Jerome up to date with the progress of his grave digging.

Ray was now thinking ahead of Jerome for the safety of his father's life. Ray knew that if he released his father, his father would implicate both him and Jerome, but time was closing in on every one of them. Ray now realized that his brother was desperate and would kill rather than be accused of raping a minor. From the stories he had heard, the inmate population of prison did not take kindly to convicted child rapists. Let alone a priest turned child rapist.

Ray made it easy on Fr. Jerome. He told him that their father had passed away in his sleep and that he, Jerome, should try to be there as soon as possible. Jerome felt more relieved than sad at the reported passing of his father. He just wanted to spend a few hours at Jimmy's house, perform the burial rights for his father in Jimmy's house then the following day or night Jimmy and Ray would dispose of the body. They were lucky that as yet the FBI was not on to Ray or Jimmy so their house was not being watched. Once again Fr. Jerome left by way of the back, disguised as a female and boarded a flight to Albany. Everything went well. They had stored the old man's body in a freezer until Jerome could arrive and Ray could complete the digging of the grave. Jerome talked to Ray for more than three hours, bringing Ray up to date about all that had transpired since their last face to face meeting.

Jerome failed to mention his telephone conversations with Cindy. He felt sure that he could take care of Cindy tonight, once and for all.

The Deadly Priest

The funeral preparations and burial services went well, in a hurried way. However, Jerome was not given the opportunity to see or spend much time with his Father's body and that seemed puzzling. His father did not look quite like himself and Jerome thought it could possibly be due to the inadequate lighting in the basement. Jerome said a hasty burial mass, shorter than usual, since he was preoccupied with his future plans now that he was in Albany.

Jerome left without telling Ray or Jimmy his next move. He told them both that he wanted to be back at the Diocese before daybreak With the FBI and other law enforcement staking out the Diocese this would be a perfect alibi for Jerome if he could return to the Diocese unnoticed, then no one would suspect him of Cindy's death.

Jerome hated to do this, but this was the only solution to this problem. He drove to Cindy's house, careful to keep his disguise as an old woman. He called her house, thirty minutes prior to his arrival there, from a pay phone. She answered; Jerome hung up and proceeded to her home. He tried the door it was unlocked. This is good he thought.

He had his Smith and Wesson thirty-eight caliber with silencer ready. He tiptoed quietly into her bedroom and there she was lying in bed covered up from head to toe. "This is good I would not have to see her open eyes in surprise and agony," he said to himself. He quickly fired two slugs in the area of her head. He was sure he had hit her for he saw the body jerk with each shot.

Jerome left in a hurry but when he got outside this

time he operated like an old lady trying to get home. One who could hardly walk. Jerome made it home the way he had left. He thought to himself all's well that ends well. He did not dispose of the gun. He took it back to the Diocese because he knew he might have uses for it again. No one knew he had left or returned. He was careful to wear gloves so that he did not leave any finger prints.

Ray and Jimmy hatched out a plan to get rid of Scar Face and Marble Eye. The plan was to plant drugs in their motel room. Ray wanted no part of those goons, let alone to go near where they stayed. Jimmy told Ray not to worry; he had people capable of taking care of that task. It had to be either Jimmy or perhaps one of the maids.

Kelly was charged, tried and convicted of drug possession and was sentenced to six months, because of her refusal to cooperate with police in their investigation of the priests kidnapping or she would have done the job planting the drugs.

The two detectives pressed charges on Kelly for drug possession hoping she would crack under pressure of the confinement. They thought she would opt for a reduced sentence, especially since she did not know James/Ray that well. But she held out.

It was not Kelly's first time in the joint and every time she found herself behind bars, she used the time to clean herself up. It always gave her the opportunity to purge herself from the drug dependency. To Kelly it was a vacation. Being locked up would hurt the detectives cause rather than help it. Kelly would remain defiant and refuse to talk.

Ray would not set foot anywhere near the goons, much less enter their rooms. James, as he now called himself, had several flashbacks since he was released from the hospital. It seemed he enjoyed his good health and was not planning to jeopardize it at this time nor at any time in the near future. His hearing had returned perfectly as his doctor had said.

It was now about six months since his encounter with the thugs and Ray would give up his life before he would relive that experience.

It would be left up to Jimmy to make and carry out such a plan. Ray was indeed trying to keep a low profile for a number of reasons. He was now wanted for questioning in the disappearance of his father and he was wanted by Scar Face and Marble Eye. The time had come for him to leave Albany as soon as possible but not before he and Jimmy would take care of the heist.

Plans were progressing nicely and they decided to do a test run of the plan one week from Thanksgiving Day. Ray's two friends from New York City would travel up to Albany a few days before Thanksgiving so as not to arouse suspicion. They chose Thanksgiving because of the busy shopping season. Jimmy transported large sums of money from banks to ATMs. Also the holiday season was one of the busiest travel seasons. It was hoped that the two robbers would blend in. They both had long rap sheets for armed robbery, racketeering, money laundering and aggravated assault, as well.

Also, they wanted some time to make themselves familiar with the area. They wanted to remain in Albany for a week.

The master plan would involve the players to be in place at the planned location, Ray would be the exception. He wanted to stay indoors as much as possible, due to the fact he was a person of interest in connection to the disappearance of the old priest and the thugs were on his heels. Ray was petrified now that Scar Face and Marble Eye were in Albany.

Since Jerome had "fine tuned" the final details, it was accepted that he knew exactly what he would have to do. On Jimmy and Ray's insistence, Fr. Jerome was considering their offer to be the getaway driver.

Jerome wanted no part of it at first, mainly because of what had taken place on his last visit to Albany. The arrangement of the heist was that Jerome would maintain his priestly appearance and that, they (the robbers) would make it appear as though he was carjacked by the robbers who held a gun to his head, and made him drive the getaway car.

There was a lot that Jerome did not tell Ray. One of the things was that he would have no explanation for being in Albany. Secondly, Jerome was not eager to go back to Albany if he could avoid it. If Jerome was willing to participate then he would have to use his disguise to leave the Diocese again. If anything went wrong it would jeopardize his airtight alibi, because he knew he was being watched. Then there would be reason to believe that he probably left the Diocese unnoticed on more than one occasion.

So, at this time, Jerome was playing it safe and listening out for the outcome of the murder investigation before he could undertake another venture. Fr. Jerome knew he had found himself on the wrong side of the law and was digging himself in deeper and deeper with each passing day.

Due to his heavy guilty feelings, he thought it was best not to be anywhere near Albany. But Ray convinced his brother using his own words on him, "You said that once our father died you wanted to switch careers." Jerome had a lot to think about these days. However, he knew he did not want to be part of that heist.

Ray, on the other hand, was not too concerned about the two thugs after him. For the moment, he thought that they did not know he was using a different name. Everyone knew him. In addition to that, no one knew he was staying at Jimmy's.

After leaving the motel with his father, Ray's whereabouts became unknown.

Jimmy solicited the assistance of a motel maid to plant four ounces of heroine in Scar Face and Marble Eye's room. The plan was for Martha, a long working reliable and efficient maid, to hide the heroine in their room. She was to let it sit for a day or two then report it to the police.

Jimmy promised her five thousand in return for the favor. Martha was happy to do so because the looks of them gave her the creeps. She was happy to see them leave at any cost.

The more Jerome thought about everything, the more he saw the perfect picture unfolding. First, he had an iron clad alibi. Since he suspected the feds were watching the Diocese he could not be suspected for the murder of Cindy.

He had secured the confidence of a millionaire parishioner who owned his own private jet and was becoming Jerome's main source of transportation. He had flown him on three trips, unaware of Jerome's duplicity. He was the getaway flier right after Jerome's visit to Cindy's apartment.

He also flew Jerome's father under the pretense that the old priest was going to Albany for specialist treatment. Jerome conned the pilot into believing that the priest and Diocese wanted the procedure to be done in complete privacy. So they would not let anyone know where he was.

This was the reason that Bob did not come forward with any information related to the old man's disappearance. Bob, the millionaire pilot, went along and said nothing.

He was well respected in Massachusetts because of his wealth. He sat on the board of three major financial institutions and no one knew how he came about his wealth. Word had it that his father was a Texas oil tycoon, others said Bob was involved with the Mob.

One thing was for sure, Bob was a womanizer and that was the reason he got his own private aircraft and that is why he flew himself. He could charm the pants off of any woman.

On his first trip to Albany, he met a beautiful woman named Laura, and his romance with her became ongoing. So even when he was not flying Jerome to Albany, he was transporting himself to see his new found love. He even used Jerome as an excuse to his wife on more than one occasion when he was going by himself. So these days, Bob was more than willing to take Jerome to Albany whenever he wanted to go.

Jerome thought things over. Perhaps he really did not want to use his disguise to leave the Diocese, once he would be traveling with Bob. But, on the other hand, the feds could track their destination. Jerome had the feeling that if something happened with the heist he might not be questioned and released at the same time. The investigators may have a reason to hold him indefinitely. He thought to himself, if he was held for any reason, then he would have to use his priestly appearance and poise to get out of that situation without being suspected as a participant.

So in Fr. Jerome's evil mind, he knew that he would orchestrate another ride to Albany the same day of the planned heist. This time he would not even need a disguise because he would be driven to the private air strip via Bob's private limo. He would participate in the heist as an unsuspecting priest and visitor to Albany. But, then he had second thoughts about the whole thing. He just did not want to be there at all.

Jerome had convoluted thoughts. Now that his father and Cindy were out of the picture, he had one last threat he wanted to take care of, and that was Bob.

Bob was a threat for more than one reason; the first was that Bob knew too much about him. Secondly,

Bob's wife had turned to Jerome for counseling because she was always having problems with her womanizing husband. Due to the constant contact with Fr. Jerome at her home and the Diocese, Mary found comfort in Jerome, not only spiritually and mentally but also physically. Jerome and Mary were now having an affair, while Bob made his trips to Albany.

Mary was only forty-seven. She could easily pass for thirty-seven whereas, Bob was in his sixties. He had never told her his correct age, perhaps he could be older. Ironically, at least on two occasions when he told her he was taking Fr. Jerome to Albany, Fr. Jerome was taking Mary, his wife, to ecstasy. Jerome was becoming fonder of Mary, so he kept thinking of a way to take care of Bob. He knew sooner or later, Bob would find out about the affair and Jerome was afraid of Bob's wealth and his connections.

Secondly, Bob knew all his whereabouts, including his connection to the disappearance of his father.

Jerome was now spending lots and lots of time with Mary. He spent a few days at the mansion when Bob went away for a week on business, culminating to a few days before Fr. Thom disappeared.

The relationship had started one Sunday at confession, after which Jerome, seeing Mary's vulnerability became a regular visitor to the mansion, under the pretence he was visiting as a priest. As the relationship developed, Mary would make trips to New York when Jerome was vacationing.

This was going on for some time before the FBI's scrutiny was on Jerome.

This explained why Jerome was taking off on such a regular basis, and also the person he claimed to stay with when his whereabouts could not be disclosed, turned out to be Mary.

Bob and Mary's marriage was a rocky one and Jerome and Mary were planning to get rid of Bob since he was now standing in the way of their romance, and happy living. Little did Mary know that Jerome had other motives as to why he wanted Bob out of the way.

Jerome thought he had the answers. He had no plans of returning to the Diocese. He would collect his portion of the heist from his brother, Bob would fly him to Nebraska where he would kill him, and then Mary would join him in Nebraska so they could start their new life. Things seemed to be working out even though Jerome did not initially plan it that way. What the heck?, he thought to himself, his father was dead and despite other circumstances, Now was the time he had earmarked to start his new life. Now was the beginning of Jerome's life which was finally taking a turn for the better. Jerome thought to himself, patience has finally paid off. Jerome knew that he had an air tight alibi since he was aware that the FBI kept constant tabs on the Diocese and no one knew that he had left that night for Albany.

He took special care to ensure he was not being followed despite his disguise. Jerome knew that only Bob could punch a hole in his alibi. But then again he was sure no one would think of questioning Bob.

CHAPTER NINE

Cindy returned from the store, not having the slightest idea of the situation she was about to face. She soon found out how quickly her life could take on a new role. She had left her friend Jasmine asleep in bed. They had planned to go out on the town, "girl's night" and they were hoping to run into Rob with his new date.

Robert who first dated Cindy and then Jasmine was having an affair with one of the girls who worked with Cindy. Jasmine confronted Rob, and a huge fight ensued so Jas, as she was called, stormed out of the apartment that they both shared and decided to spend the night with Cindy.

When Cindy first saw the blood on the bed she immediately became hysterical. She started to scream and call out her friend's name. She was optimist, hoping for a reply. What she saw, she hoped she would never in her life see again. Lying in her bed was Jasmine just as she left her, with two gun shots to her head. Cindy leaned on the wall to prevent herself from passing out. Her first thoughts were of Robert.

What a monster he was, to do something so out of character. She knew him for quite some time and found it difficult to comprehend such a callous act. Rob always seemed so polite. He also seemed to be a non-violent person. Why would Rob want to kill her if their relationship was at the end? Cindy remembered something Rob had told her when they broke up, that somehow there would be a better man out there for her.

Now look what misfortune had befallen her friend at his hands. What Cindy did not know was that her friend was at the wrong place at the wrong time. Cindy did not hesitate any longer. She called 911.

The coroner pronounced her best friend dead at the scene, Cindy's house was now a crime scene and she knew full well that she could be considered a prime suspect and come under scrutiny. Cindy knew that things would not look good for her since there was no forced entry and that she did not have an alibi for the time the murder took place. She knew that it all happened in the space of a few minutes. She was not gone for thirty minutes for sure. She was very nervous that no one would believe her story.

The killing had made the news, but Ray did not even give it a thought. At that time, Ray was totally unaware of who was behind the murder.

The following day, Fr. Jerome learned through Ray of the murder of someone close to Cindy, at Cindy's home. Jerome was dumbfounded. Jerome called Ray from a pay phone as always, expecting to hear of Cindy's death only to find out that he had killed the wrong person. Jerome now realized he had made a deadly mistake.

The Deadly Priest

Jerome did not even let Ray know what he had done. He just walked around the Diocese for the next few days, dazed as if he were in a trance. Members of the Diocese were aware of his strange behavior and relieved him of his duties, until he could get himself together. Some of the clergy blamed the sudden change in his behavior on the disappearance of his father. In his quiet moments he thought, eventually Cindy would be blamed for her friend's death, since there was no forced entry. It would be very difficult for her to explain the circumstances of this situation.

There was yet another factor that would work against poor Cindy to which Jerome had no knowledge. Cindy used to date Rob, a year or two before Jasmine. Everyone knew that to be a fact. A few women found it odd, understanding how Cindy was okay with her friend dating a man she once dated. The detectives went to work on Cindy asking her numerous questions over and over again to confirm her story and as a means of finding out if she would change her story.

Cindy was becoming, nervous and scared, and impatient that the detectives would think she had in fact killed her friend in a jealous rage.

In the meantime, they also had Rob in custody for questioning. Rob had an alibi; he had spent the night in the company of his new found lover. She confirmed that they spent the night dancing at a club then they arrived home at three am. She stated that Rob was always in her presence since he arrived at her home at eight pm. The murder of Jasmine took place between nine and nine thirty pm. Rob was indeed in the clear so all attention was focused on Cindy as the investigation continued.

Jimmy now relied solely on Ray to create and carry out all of the final planning of the robbery. Ray was now spending his time exclusively at Jimmy's home. He stayed indoors working out the final details of the heist.

On certain days, Jimmy usually transported new notes along with used notes. The used notes usually were twice as much as the new ones. Ray knew that older notes were harder to trace because they were no longer in sequence like the newer ones. Ray completed the final plot for the heist to take place on the day Jimmy was carrying more old than new notes.

The plan to get rid of Scar Face and Marble Eye was also being worked out. But somehow, Scar Face and Marble were able to find Jimmy's house, while Jimmy was at work, thanks to Jimmy's creation. Ray heard the thugs were in the neighborhood asking around the previous night. This was why the plan to get rid of them was on high alert. Number one on Jimmy's list of priorities was in fact that he did not want to see any harm come to his friend, the mastermind of the heist.

It was around three pm. Jimmy had just awakened to the sound of a crash at the front door. The two thugs were trying to force their way in. Ray saw them on the camera Jimmy had installed. Despite their size and weight, the door would not budge. They would need a rammer like the swat team uses to gain entry.

Ray was not about to wait around to find out. He hid behind a secret double wall Jimmy had constructed for hiding illegal drugs and any contraband should the cops raid his house at anytime. It was specifically designed for that purpose.

The double wall led down into a small section of the basement which was cut off from the rest of the room and made to look like it was part of the furnace. Lady luck was with Ray. He was happy now that Jimmy had let him in on this secret hiding place.

Ray could hear them talking outside. He could not quite make out what they were saying, but the sound of their voices made him relive his night of horror six months ago. He felt pretty sure his end was near, despite being in the safety of his hiding place. Ray felt so scared, it was as though he wanted to go outside and make a run for it. In his estimation they were no less than thirty feet away from where he sat on the inside.

Ray had flashbacks of the beating he suffered at the hands of those two thugs. He was also angry and enraged to be so close to them. He thought of revenge but knew he was no match for one of them much less two. He knew this time, if they found him, they would definitely kill him on sight.

Ray knew the only way to beat those goons, he would have to kill them with a gun like a sniper, because they were packing also, and no one knew their shooting capability.

Jimmy had installed a silent alarm system that transmitted a signal to his beepers once that secret part of the house was entered. Jimmy was now aware of entry. He knew something was going on. Could it be someone strange or was it Ray searching for something. Ray has never ventured in that area for the past three months he stayed there. The real reason for the alarm and camera was that Jimmy was a big time drug dealer. He only drove the armored car as a front, not to arouse suspicion, but he didn't trust Ray or anyone to be among his stash for any reason.

Since he lived by himself, the alarm was intended to let him know if and when his stash was being violated.

Anything or anyone short of the police would have a rude awakening if they showed up at Jimmy's house unannounced and unwelcomed. Jimmy showed Ray the access door just in case an emergency like this one should crop up. Jimmy kept Ray happy with an adequate supply of drugs, so there was no necessity for Ray to enter his secret domain. Jimmy called his house but there was no answer so he became worried.

Was there a bust going down? It was highly unlikely because Jimmy only did wholesale business with ex-cons he knew and he had a very clean operation for the past seven years.

He had a premonition something was wrong, Jimmy liked Ray because he knew Ray was smart. He thought to himself that he had uses for Ray somewhere along the line because he was impressed with Ray's planning and his keen interest. But in order to protect his friend, first, he had to get rid of those thugs who were asking around for him. Jimmy knew those thugs would stop at nothing until they got their man so he surely had to implement his plan ASAP.

The Deadly Priest

The two thugs left right after the phone rang. They knew that they might have triggered a silent alarm, trying to break in the front door and that cops could arrive within minutes. What they did not know was that it was Jimmy who called to see if everything was okay at his home and the last thing Jimmy wanted at his home were cops.

Jimmy diverted from his scheduled route to make sure all was well at his home. He found Ray shaken and scared but nonetheless happy to see him. Ray told Jimmy what had transpired and they both decided that somehow they had to get rid of those two thugs in order to implement their planned heist.

While the thugs were visiting Jimmy's home in search of Ray, Martha implemented the first part of the plan to frame them. Plan B would be new notes from the heist.

Ray's two friends from New York arrived and Jimmy showed them around for a few days. They rented a car and made themselves familiar with the getaway route to the point of the rendezvous.

They practiced the getaway run for seven days before the final move was rehearsed. If all went well the heist would be seven days from the final practice. For obvious reasons the two new comers never saw Ray nor did they know Jimmy's correct name.

He told them his nickname was Bolt.

The thugs, Scar Face and Marble, returned to their motel room as if nothing ever happened, but were a bit surprised to find their maid in a little friendly spirit. She always seemed to be unhappy, as though she did not enjoy what she was doing, and always seemed to be in a hurry to leave, even if she had not completed her task.

What brought about that sudden change was any one's guess. Or maybe she was happy to find out they had informed management they would be leaving within three days.

Martha informed Jimmy of this new development, Jimmy thanked her and informed Ray.

Jimmy told Martha to hold off on the police report since they were soon leaving but if they did not leave within the time frame, she should execute the plan.

CHAPTER TEN

The investigation had intensified. Cindy and Robert became prime suspects. There were no witnesses to place Fr. Jerome at the scene of the crime. His disguise worked perfectly and any passerby would not even think that an old lady going about her business could have any significant impact on a homicide investigation.

Father Jerome was literally getting away with murder. The cops for some reason did not believe Cindy's story. Why should they?

It seemed to them she was hiding something to protect her ex-lover, how convenient it seemed that she had just stepped out long enough for her best friend to get whacked. Then, she returned to call 911 with the body still warm as an alibi to cover both herself and her ex. Detectives quizzed both Rob and Cindy for more than seventy two hours focusing on their alibis.

No finger prints of Rob were found at the crime scene, but numerous prints of Cindy's were lifted which did not prove anything since she lived there. Cindy and Rob went over their stories of their activities leading up to the time of the murder maybe a hundred times or more.

Detectives attentive to details were looking out for any slight change. There was nothing that they could pinpoint on either Rob or Cindy, so they let them go, instructing them both not to leave Albany unless they notified the police department. They were now considered prime suspects for the murder of Jasmine Alinter.

As the day of the heist grew closer, big questions remained. Should they wait it out and do the heist a week later? Ray went back to the drawing board. He concluded that perhaps the heist should take place on the same day the thugs were due to leave, this way it would cast suspicion on them and the cops in New York will keep an eye on them. Ray's number one motive was revenge. He knew that the plan for the heist now had to be moved up a few days to the day the two thugs were scheduled to leave.

The thugs left Albany for New York earlier than planned. They were called back to attend to another contract that needed their immediate attention. It would be a shock to everyone concerned. Not even Martha, the maid, knew about this new development and would only find out from her supervisor when she returned to work.

It was as though the thugs sensed trouble. But that was not the case. In their line of business, they were always busy. Sometimes one visit from them would be all that was needed. It didn't always go the way things went with their search for Ray. The thugs were upset that Ray had given them the run around. The day before the heist, Ray's two friends relaxed and watched a movie. Jimmy went about his business as usual. The plot was indeed perfect, only Jimmy and Ray knowing the final details.

It would no longer be necessary for Fr. Jerome to drive the getaway car. Just Ray's two friends Paul and John would be needed, along with Jimmy playing the role of the innocent armored car driver.

The time of the heist was gradually approaching and all the plans were in place. Paul and John had not yet seen Ray. Ray wanted to remain out of sight of these two would be robbers for fear that if things did not work out he would be implicated. However, he did speak to them from a pay phone. The plan was for Ray to leave Albany two days before the heist, for Massachusetts, to join Jerome. Since they were identical twins they hoped to switch identity briefly. In order to make this exchange possible Jerome left for awhile pretending to visit Mary, at the mansion.

Ray was already there and only Mary knew what was going on. Her husband was pretty sure it was Fr. Jerome he was looking at. The identity switch had to take place away from the church for obvious reasons. The two men spoke briefly and Bob left the mansion to attend to some urgent business. This time, Mary knew where he was headed and why. Mary was not supposed to know about the plans but Fr. Jerome let her know anyway.

These days, Mary was hoping that Bob would get caught with whatever he was doing so she could get rid of him for a few years. Bob was an indirect participant in the robbery; his plane would transport the loot to Ray in Massachusetts. As it was, he still did not know that Ray was in Albany, let alone in Massachusetts. Bob was not aware of the heist. All that he knew was that he would meet with Martha to collect a large sum of money.

Ray changed into Jerome's priest garments and Jerome, feeling like a free man, checked into a five star hotel in New York City. Mary came along for the ride posing as Mrs. Wharton.

The new plans for the heist were that neither Ray nor Jerome would be in Albany at the time of the heist.

Jerome always thought ahead of his brother, after all Jerome was the smarter of the twins. Ray would have no alibi since he had replaced Jerome at the Diocese. Ray returned to the Diocese under the watchful eyes of the surveillance camera, if there was really one. No one ever knew it was Ray at the Diocese and not Jerome.

It really would not be too difficult to fake Fr. Jerome. His duties had not been restored and prior to the day of the heist, Jerome made his act outstanding to ensure he did not receive his duties. Now, all Ray had to do was follow along the lines Jerome was playing. Their meticulous plan worked. No one in the Diocese knew Ray was not Jerome.

The week of Thanksgiving started like a typical fall day. The beautiful fall colors and the damp cloudy atmosphere blended with the occasional cool breezes and falling leaves. The change of the weather was a welcome relief to most people after a sweltering hot summer. The temperatures would be in the seventies all day. No one had the slightest idea of the events to come.

They already had an unsolved murder and public opinion varied. As a matter of fact it was the talk of the town. Cindy and Rob were already tried and found guilty in the court of public opinion. The general view was mixed; some said it was Rob, some said Cindy was an active participant.

Jimmy arrived for work as usual. He was a bit tensed but tried to hide his anxiety from his work mates by singing. To his co-workers this was not unusual because Jimmy was always this happy after a big drug deal. Of course, he never told them why he seemed happy at times. He took the usual route he had been doing for more than one year.

The stops were all the same only varying from day to day. Jimmy was thanking his lucky stars that most armored cars in Albany were single occupancy. He had no partner. It was that way for two reasons: one to save the company an extra pay check and secondly there had been no armored car heists for more than twenty years in this peaceful town.

He had the most important part of the plan to implement. Jimmy's first stop was always for gas. Everything was routine to the uncaring observer.

Jimmy made his way into the store and accidentally bumped into Martha. A few thousand new bank notes with serial numbers in sequence fell into Martha's oversized pocket book. Jimmy was carrying money for the gas station in the usual bag, but had ten thousand dollars in brand new notes, concealed until that accidental bump occurred.

Now Martha must somehow find a way to deliver these notes to Scar Face and Marble's room. They would leave tomorrow at eleven. It was now nine am. Martha seemed pretty confident she could manage her task at hand. However, she was still not aware the two goons had checked out already.

Next stop for Jimmy would be the check cashing store. There Jimmy left an unusually large sum of money, but then again no one except Jimmy and the guys that ran the twenty four hour cashier knew what amount of money Jimmy normally left there. Usually it would be enough cash for at least twenty four hours. But on weekends they would have money for at least seventy two hours, mostly used bank notes.

Martha retrieved the extra three million dollars left there for her to pick up from the dumpster at the back of the check cashing office.

By eleven a.m. Jimmy got the beep he was waiting for. Martha had been successful in planting the money. Or so she led him to believe, because the thugs had already left on a nine am flight to New York City, even before Martha collected the ten thousand. But Martha had other ideas of her own, because Martha was a casual heroine user.

Somehow she maintained control of her weekend usage and used at the rate she could afford. She was always able to maintain her job in order to maintain her habit. Now she had heroine and ten thousand dollars cash. Martha was suspicious that she might not be paid, so now that the thugs were gone, Martha decided the dope and money would be hers.

She delivered the three money bags she retrieved from the dumpster to a person that seemed familiar to her. He was a regular guest to the hotel with a woman these days, he said he was from out of town but it seemed that he spent more time with that woman than he spent time where he lived.

Jimmy rolled into super Mart #2. This was to be a pick up. He had done most of his drop offs. All that remained was two million dollars in new notes. Jimmy knew where he had to stop, he also knew he would be struck from behind, but he never saw John or Paul, nor did he see what hit him.

The two men drove the armored car around to the back. They quickly transferred what was left to their rental van, which was not part of the plan, and headed for nearby interstate eighty-one. Things were going well for the robbers, "too good to be true," said John to Paul, "did they really think we would give them a share of our loot? After all, they just planned this thing, I am glad Ray was not in with us, did he think we were going to share our loot because of his ingenious plan."

"We are rich" blurted Paul.

They were headed to the rest area fifteen minutes away which was designated the rendezvous point to change their vehicle if nothing unexpected happened.

Onlookers, who witnessed this incident, called 911

and gave a complete description of the two men, the plate number, color, make and model of the rental van.

In less than two minutes, at least one unmarked police cruiser was on to them. The cops knew where they were headed from a tip they had received a few minutes prior to the robbery. They were just following along to make sure the two robbers followed the tipster's information.

After a few maneuvers to make sure they were not being followed, the two robbers headed to the rendezvous point. What they did not know was that there were several unmarked police cars in radio contact following them. They were confident they were home free, since they were sure that they were not being followed. They made it safely to the rest area without any incident, without any helicopter overhead. This was indeed the easiest FIVE MIL JOB!!!!!

Or so they thought.

Expecting Ray at the next rest area, their plan was to kill Ray, so that he or his friend, the armored car driver, would not have a share in the loot. It was developing to be a double cross situation. Their plan for Jimmy after they left Albany safely, would be to let the cops know that it was an inside job and Jimmy was involved.

Once Ray and Jimmy were out of the way, the two men would each get to keep two point five million. They found their way without any problems to the vehicle where Ray was supposed to be waiting. They approached the vehicle cautiously, guns drawn but concealed from prying eyes. They reached the blue van with engine running as was the plan. They simultaneously reached for the back door of the van, yanked it open only to find themselves staring down the barrels of six semi-automatic weapons owned by New York state police. It seemed like cops came from everywhere.

Paul and John were arrested without a fight and charged with armed robbery. It seemed that they were double crossed; Ray was not even in Albany. The two robbers never had a chance at the real loot. The real loot was already airborne.

Paul and John were set up by Ray and Jimmy to play off the real heist. It was an ingenious plan for them to be found with at least some of the cash new notes and all with serial numbers in sequence. The remainder had just touched down in Lowell, Massachusetts.

Paul and John were transported separately. They did use their Miranda right, the right to remain silent.

After several weeks of investigations and intense questioning, Cindy and Rob were charged with murder in the first degree. Since the truth was not forthcoming from either Cindy or Rob, the cops charged both of them with the hope that the two defendants would start pointing fingers at each other and the truth would finally come out.

The District Attorney knew that their case was very weak. Even though they had a murder on their hands they could not place Cindy or Rob at the scene of the crime. They both had alibis that were thoroughly checked out. If their case went to trial, the case would hinge on circumstantial evidence. Rob and Cindy were arraigned a few weeks after Jasmine's funeral.

Prior to being formally charged, both Rob and Cindy had consented to a lie detector test. Both tests were returned inconclusive, so the detectives knew that they had very little to go on.

They decided to gamble that Cindy's confinement would bring about a break in this murder investigation, that Cindy would crack under pressure and give up Rob as the trigger man. After a few days in confinement the investigators offered Cindy a deal, to give evidence against Rob because they felt sure Cindy had a hand in this murder and was protecting Rob. The lead detective wanted Cindy to say she saw Rob leaving the scene when she returned from the store.

Even though Cindy thought it had to be Rob that killed her best friend, Cindy did not see him, so she did not want to lie. Even though it might make her position better, in her mind it was difficult to tell if the cops would let her go once she told that lie. Cindy continued to claim her innocence and told the cops there was really nothing she could offer that would help the investigators. Cindy insisted that she was not there when her friend was killed, but would be more than happy when the cops found out who the real killer was.

The media covered the funeral, also the arraignment. It was a media frenzy, the headlines read: "Nabbed".

"Love triangle accused killers face the judge": "Triangle killers have their day in court". Three is a crowd etc!

Cindy was more than embarrassed to be led away in handcuffs on national TV. She was humiliated and wished she had not left her friend that day to go to the store. Cindy doubted Rob's innocence, seems that Rob waited for that unguarded moment to make his move. Oh! If only she had a glimpse of him that fateful night, it would be all the proof she needed. She thought to herself, who, other than Rob, would want Jas dead? Cindy did not even realize how close she had come to being killed. It didn't occur to her that the killer wanted her dead instead of Jasmine.

These days Cindy did not have the time to think or reflect on the Diocese. Cindy and Rob both had public defenders. Cindy's lawyer told her that the prosecution had a very weak case and that she would be home soon. So weak was their case, said the public defender Harry Druid, that the case might not even go to trial due to insufficient evidence.

"All they have is a body, they have no murder weapon, no finger prints except yours and you live there. No eyewitness to the crime. Their case had no merit," he went on to say "Jas could have been killed by a drifter."

Even though the police would not entertain that theory, Harry Druid told Cindy that had this not been an election year the investigation would still be ongoing rather than charges being filed this early in the investigation. He assured her, that based on the evidence they provided due to DISCOVERY, with what they had, they would not be able to prove their case.

Cindy and Rob remained in custody, without bail pending the outcome of the murder investigation.

The Albany police were all of a sudden up against a sudden surge of crime. Three major crimes in the past few months; two unsolved crimes, one potential kidnapping and suspected murder along with an armored car heist, never heard of in more than three decades.

The Albany Police and FBI were more than grateful for the tips that led to the apprehension of the two armored car suspects. At least they had this heist partially solved. The investigation was far from being completed, but at least they had something to start with.

Since the two robbers were from out of town, the FBI was focusing on visitors to Albany over the past two weeks. That, in itself, would be a daunting task considering the heist took place during the busiest travel time of the year, Thanksgiving. Airlines and hotels were always sold out at that time of year.

It would be an impossible task to go over all those records, maybe the investigators would have no choice but to narrow it down to the week of Thanksgiving, then work their way out if nothing was relevant to the investigation.

First came the disappearance of Fr. Thom. The police had enough DNA to prove he stayed in a motel in Albany before he disappeared without a trace. His son was considered a person of interest in his disappearance. Despite his DNA being present in the motel in Albany, that was not enough to prove he kidnapped his father. The detectives needed more before they could charge a priest with anything. It is not every day that a priest is accused of kidnapping, and of his father, at that. As the facts stood, it could only be treated as an alleged kidnapping.

So far his whereabouts were still unknown. Therefore, his disappearance was still being treated as a missing person. Fr. Jerome had retained an attorney and was no longer talking to the police. It is suspicious when a family member hires an attorney so that they can remain quiet, rather than cooperate with investigators to solve a crime perpetrated against a loved one. Then on the heels of Fr. Thom's disappearance, followed a real murder mystery with almost nothing to go on except a body, the death of Jasmine. Then, as if that was not enough for investigators in less than two weeks, followed the armored car heist.

There was a great outcry from the Clergy, members of the community and politicians for a speedy resolution of these crimes, especially the kidnapping and possible murder of a priest.

The morale among detectives would soon hit an all time low with mounting pressure from the media.

The District Attorney himself held a press conference to appeal to members of the public for help to solve these three important cases; an unsolved murder, a suspected love triangle gone bad, followed by an armored car heist. Even though two of the robbers were apprehended red handed with the cash in hand, more than half of the funds taken from the armored car were not recovered. The cops were looking at the possibility of an inside job. Jimmy was under intense questioning and scrutiny.

The DA was offering up to ten thousand dollars for information that would lead to the arrest and prosecution of the perpetrators of these criminal acts.

Cindy was about to put pieces together in her own way. She had the pieces correctly but did not know she did. She asked herself over and over again did this all have anything to do with Hector the investigator. Would that bit of information be helpful? Was it of any significance? She thought to herself she should at least let her Attorney know. What if Hector was the killer? This idea seemed remote but nevertheless she would discuss it with her lawyer when he came to visit her again because the lawyer was leaning to a drifter theory.

Cindy thought things over and the more she thought about the drifter theory, the more things seemed to make sense, if her imagination was not getting the better of her. On the other hand, Cindy was not sure she wanted to add to the embarrassment of being labeled an extortionist. Once she brought out Hector then Fr. Jerome would not hesitate to make her look like an extortionist. All the odds seemed that it would be better for her not to mention what she thought might have a profound impact against her in the public's eye. Who would believe what had transpired in her life over the past six to eight months. She knew that she was on to something. But now she was sitting in jail, with limited use of a phone. She was still a bit timid to tell her lawyer her story for fear that Jerome would accuse her of extortion, but on the other hand, could he prove it? Chances were, who would now believe an accused murderer over a priest?

Even though Cindy was only arraigned, it seemed as though she was already found guilty for something she did not do. She knew no one wanted to believe her innocence and in the eyes of some members of the public, she was already guilty. She knew it would be difficult to have a fair trial.

Cindy wanted now, more than ever, to keep the sexual assault at the Diocese a secret. She never intended for it to go to court anyway. She just saw it as an opportunity to make some extra money.

She was already becoming mindful of the media. Cindy knew they would feast on that incident to make her look even worse than she really was. Then the scandal of Fr. Thom's infidelity, that leads up to the possibility of him being her father. Imagine a priest guilty of incest. It would make a great headline story.

Cindy was pretty sure that after Jerome had gotten rid of his father, he would make sure every shred of evidence of that assault no longer existed. But she was more concerned with the extortion she could be charged with, and the possibility that Jerome could possibly be her brother.

The Deadly Priest

CHAPTER ELEVEN

Part Two

Jerome was awakened from a deep sleep. The circumstances surrounding his awakening were difficult and confusing. Jerome could not believe what was happening to him. He was pretty sure he was dreaming?

It was his father standing over him shaking him awake.

Jerome, in his boyhood days, had heard several ghost stories and as a priest believed in the death and resurrection of Jesus Christ. But never could he imagine his father returning from the dead. He just could not figure out what was happening. His first thought was that he had gotten rid of Cindy only to find out Cindy was still alive and unharmed and her friend was dead instead. Then he said a prayer and buried his father and now he was also alive. Jerome was sure he was dreaming and having a nightmare. In the past he knew when he had bad dreams he would say to himself "you're dreaming" and awake from the nightmare. But now it was different and Jerome purposely rolled over so he could actually touch his father's hand. He felt as though his father was standing in the flesh, alive and well and speaking to him.

It was difficult to understand what was happening. His father had arisen from the dead.

Fr. Thomas was now standing over Jerome shaking him awake. Jerome could not understand if he, himself was dead or alive because he thought his father was dead and buried. Jerome's first thought was to come awake slowly giving himself time to think. Was he dreaming? Where was he? What was going on was difficult for him to comprehend. There were many reasons that he did not want to be awake fully, just yet. Nothing made sense to him. Did he not go to Albany and say a prayer for his father's burial. The only thing being that he didn't actually see him buried but he was sure his father was dead. Didn't he take care of Cindy? Or was that in his dreams as well? Where was Ray? What had happened to Cindy? What was happening? Jerome couldn't answer any of his own questions.

Fr. Thom said to Fr. Jerome "Son you have slept for almost twenty four hours."

Jerome had a hard time figuring out what was a dream and what was real. Was the heist real or was that a dream also?

Meanwhile, the prosecution case is that Cindy was in love with Rob at one time, then after they broke up Rob started seeing Jasmine. The prosecution is also alleging that Cindy never forgave her friend for taking her ex because she was still in love with him. So she waited patiently for the opportunity to get back at Jasmine. Under the guise of Jasmine's best friend she got all the first hand information of their relationship.

The media claimed that Rob was seeing Cindy at the time of the murder and they worked out a plan to get rid of Jasmine once and for all.

Fr. Thom could not wait for Jerome to gather his composure. He had waited for more than a day to break the news about Cindy to Jerome.

Jerome finally collected himself and said," father, I am amazed at your knowledge and interest in Cindy, but what has she got to do with us except that she is blackmailing us."

His father seemed all forgiving. He did not speak to his son in an angry way or with any aggression, and that had Jerome puzzled as well. Fr. Thom just calmly said, "Son, something terrible has happened", as if once again reading Jerome's mind. "Someone tried to kill Cindy. Fortunately, she is still alive but she is being considered a suspect in the death of her friend. She has formally been charged along with an ex-lover in the death of her friend, Jasmine."

"It appears that the person killed her friend instead of her".

Fr. Thom could not withhold his theory. Jerome was the only person he could confide this information to.

In Jerome's mind, Fr. Thom was back from the grave and was still preoccupied with Cindy. He went on, "she claims that her friend was killed in her apartment while she went out to buy cigarettes. Her friend was staying with Cindy at the time. Their plan was to go out to the club and her friend would stay overnight at Cindy's," Fr. Thom went on and on about the prosecution's case.

"I would like more than ever to help her in any way I can." Fr. Thom continued. Jerome was becoming sick to his stomach with disgust, now that he had just found out that he accidentally killed an innocent person, someone who had nothing to do with this situation and Cindy was alive and well at the expense of her friend. Jerome realized that this situation was no dream but was in fact a nightmare in reality. Jerome still could not understand what was happening, but decided to try something anyway. "Father, tell me, why do you continue to insist on petting a blackmailer? She did receive a settlement from the church with an agreement that nothing more should be done or said in this matter."

"Son, I am sure when I let you knew what I know at that time, you will understand what is going on. Be patient with me until you are fully awake and aware of what is taking place before you make a judgment.

Fr. Thom was finding it difficult to explain to his son that Cindy's mother Olga had now entered the picture and was now demanding that Fr. Thom help his daughter Cindy. This is how Fr. Thom was made aware of all that was going on in Cindy's life.

Olga had just come home from doing five years in jail for armed robbery a week or so before Cindy's arrest and subsequent arraignment. Olga was released on good behavior after spending five years in jail. She had been involved in an armed bank robbery due to her crack addiction. She was the getaway driver of a botched bank robbery.

Fr. Thom was never sure he fathered Cindy, but to avoid arguments and publicity at that time he decided to keep the situation under wraps. But now he had this situation to deal with again.

Jerome's heart was racing. He knew that he would have to deal with his father first, regardless. There was still a lot Jerome really could not understand. He literally pinched himself, to ensure or to reassure himself he was not dreaming, and then once again turned to face his assumed dead father.

"Father, there is really a lot that needs to be addressed. First, please let me know what you plan to do now for your precious little blackmailer."

Fr. Thom was a bit resentful but resorted to playing the patient role rather than going on the offensive. He knew he had to explain his long held secret, in order for his son to understand."Son" he went on "I did something that I do regret tremendously, similar to your situation and I have had my regrets ever since. The only difference was that I was not involved with a minor." Jerome started to say something, but his father stopped him in mid sentence. "I didn't mean it the way you are taking it, I just wanted you to know that I am being accused of fathering Cindy."

That was a bomb shell to Jerome, hearing it from his father's mouth under these extreme circumstances. Jerome was still hoping he was dreaming, and that the death of his father and that everything associated with Cindy was all a dream.

Fr. Jerome was slowly returning to the reality that

his father was never kidnapped and that all his supposed conversation with Cindy was part of his elaborate dream. He now realized that he never spoke to Cindy except when he visited her job disguised.

Fr. Thom went on, "My dear son please understand that I know now and I knew then, I had done your mother wrong, and now I would like to apologize, however, I feel one hundred percent sure that Cindy is not my child.

"But just think what we have to lose if I should have to leave this Diocese disgraced, I would not be able to keep the settlement a secret. Then what we are trying to avoid regarding your situation, might well get out into the open. You know the ramification of that situation is jail time and that is what I am trying to avert.

"Just imagine now what the media frenzy would be like after hearing this information. Her mother is now threatening to go with this information to the press if we do not help Cindy. She has assured me that once her daughter gets a good attorney the settlement agreement stands..She thinks that I am in control of the church funds so it will be easy for us to get her the best lawyer in the State of New York."

Suddenly, a sense of shock overcame Jerome he could not believe what he was hearing, was all this real? Was his father brought back from the dead to continue to torment him? Did his father ever die? He stood staring at his father perplexed. Was Cindy then really his sister and his father never let that be known until now? There were so many unanswered questions that Jerome needed time by himself, to work things out, for his own sanity. He was at a loss trying to figure out what was his dream, or what was real, but first he must find Ray. Ray held the answers to many of Jerome's questions.

Jerome rushed to the phone and started to dial every phone number he could possibly remember to contact Ray. No longer cautious that the phones might be bugged Jerome threw all caution to the wind, because he suddenly realized he had dreamt most of the investigation and questioning. He was now desperate to understand what was going on. He knew he could not ask his father to explain, and with each passing moment the more frustrated he became.

Each call he made he was told that Ray was not seen or heard from for some time.

Jerome was more confused. He felt sure he did go to Albany to say mass at his father's funeral, yet nothing seemed unusual. Even his father did not seem like he had ever left the Diocese. But he was somewhat puzzled at the way in which Ray acted when it came time for him to see his father for the last time.

It was difficult to accept that it was all a dream but the more he thought about it, the more the dream angle seemed to make sense to him In his dream, Jerome now reflected that Ray made it seem that his father's body was so badly decomposed that he did not look the same. Despite being told the body was refrigerated. He was also told that in the absence of a mortician the body was not properly prepared. Little did Jerome know that, in actuality, his brother would never see harm come to their father or participate in the kidnap and death of his father despite the circumstances of their past relationship. So Jerome figured that Ray arranged to have his father disappear and show up at the motel to convince Jerome he was kidnapped. Did this really happen or did it not?

Jerome continued to speculate putting his own twist to things right or wrong. He surmised that "once I left Albany my guess is Ray let our father stay with Jimmy for another week, arranged to buy a cadaver that fitted our father's description then called me to let me know he was dead." In his evil dream he figured that Ray made numerous excuses for the reason why their father's appearance looked different. In hindsight, Jerome now knew that nobody was bought or buried and his father never disappeared or ever left the Diocese. His father's disappearance was a dream that appeared to Jerome to be real.

The stresses of Cindy's calls were taking a profound toll on Jerome, to the extent that he seemed to be losing his mind.

Ray was linked to drugs and prostitution, but never wanted to be responsible for his father's death, despite all that had transpired in the past. Despite all the suffering, the beatings, at the hands of his father and the beatings he gave his mother, Ray would still refuse to participate in his own father's demise and be a participant to his murder.

Jerome continued to search his mind. Now he knew it was possible the heist did happen? Or was that part of his elaborate dream also. His turmoil continued. "I am pretty sure it did happen in reality, I am sure that Ray took the money and ran." There were more questions than answers. Jerome felt like he would explode for want of answers to these all important questions. He became pretty sure that in some way Ray had double crossed him. Jerome became angry and at the same time desperate for revenge. He was also forced to accept the fact that his father was indeed very much alive.

Ray became the mastermind and most wanted man. Ray just added another person or persons to the list of people who were desperately searching for him. Once Ray collected the loot in Albany, he convinced Mary to go with him. Ray started to see Mary unknown to Jerome, since Jerome could not leave the Diocese on a daily basis due to his pretense of insanity.

Mary grew tired of Bob's infidelity along with the fact that Bob was in deep financial trouble. To add to the list of Bob's troubles, Bob and May were living their own separate lives. They had not slept together in months since he met Laura in Albany. Bob's focus was on Laura. He showered her with expensive gifts and dinners in high class restaurants in New York and Las Vegas.

Once Mary started sleeping with Ray, thinking it to be Jerome, she began to think of a divorce or a way to get rid of Bob. Mary did realize a slight change in her lovemaking with Ray but could not figure out what had brought about the sudden change.

Eventually Ray had no choice but to let her know he was not Jerome. He reassured her that he was in love with her and wanted her to elope to Ohio with him to start a new life with the money from the heist.

The whole event was a total shock but by this time Mary preferred Ray's lovemaking over Jerome anyway. She told Ray she would give it serious thought and within forty-eight hours she made her decision to leave Bob for Ray.

Ray transported the loot by road. He rented a minivan, using one of Mary's credit cards and was careful to drive at the speed limit. He also ensured all the lights and turn signals on the rental vehicle worked fine, so there would be no cause to be stopped by the cops.

Everything seemed to be moving well. Ray made it to Ohio without any incident.

Jimmy was still under investigation for his part in the heist. The feds ran a check on Jimmy and found out about his criminal background. It was amazing to find out how he got hired for the job with his criminal history, even though he had worked for the armored car company for more than five years, incident free. The investigators concluded it was only a matter of time before a set up like this one took place. They concluded Jimmy was just waiting for the right time to strike.

The investigators were baffled that, since they were on to the robbers so quickly after the heist, all of the money should have been recovered, yet when they found John and Paul the two disciples, they were found with less than half the amount of money, prompting the investigators to believe that the heist was a well planned inside job. They concluded that Jimmy had something to do with it, therefore; he would be their prime target of the investigation.

The Deadly Priest

A search warrant was issued to search Jimmy's home and vehicle, somehow Jimmy stayed ahead of the investigators. A day before the heist he transferred his drugs to a friend's house an ex-con. They buried the drugs at an isolated location and Jimmy took care to clean his secret room thoroughly.

The investigators found the secret room but nothing pertaining to the robbery was recovered.

Meanwhile, Martha was living it up on the ten thousand she was supposed to plant in the thug's room. Martha was smarter than Ray or Jimmy could imagine, once she realized that the two criminals were gone before she could plant the money from the heist. Martha recovered the drugs from the motel room, and then she traded the ten thousand to a fence, who offered eight thousand for her ten thousand in new notes. Martha was careful not to deposit the money into the bank in large quantities; her salary went to the bank via direct deposit so now she was not spending her salary. She was paying for everything in cash.

Martha was following the news on television and in the newspapers. She was well aware that Jimmy was in custody and Ray might be on the run from the scene of the crime with the money from the heist, perhaps in another state.

Jimmy hired an attorney and was no longer cooperating with the police. But charges were pending for identity theft; Jimmy Dunson for the past five years was using his dead brother's identification. The feds found this out because of actual finger prints that Jimmy's first name was Fred and not Jimmy. So that explained why no one was aware that Jimmy as he called himself was a convicted felon, because, in fact, his dead brother was not.

The two armored car robbers were preparing to go on trial. They were mad because they had been set up, but they were not yet ready to cooperate with the cops. They were arraigned and subsequently indicted for armed robbery.

The DA was willing to cut them a deal for information about the heist but John and Paul remained tight lipped. Being ex-cons themselves, they knew not to be rats.

In the meantime, investigators were working feverishly on hotels and motels registration due to limited resources. It was no surprise that, after about three weeks, the cops came up with information about the thugs. A check of the airlines confirmed that they had left Albany on the day of the robbery. The rental car company provided investigators with a copy of Chuck's driver's license.

Fortunately or unfortunately, when investigators knocked on his door in New York City Chuck had moved from that address a year ago but never took the trouble to change his license to his new address. So the investigators would have to work harder now to find him.

Bob returned home after spending a week with his new found love, only to find a note that said Mary was away visiting relatives in New Haven and would not be back for another week. Bob was indeed happy to be free of Mary overlooking his every move; his first thought was to return to Laura.

Bob called and Laura told him he was always welcome whenever possible

The following day Bob was back in Laura's arms. She loved the special attention bestowed on her; she was never treated like this by anyone.

Meanwhile Ray, with his new found love Mary, was living it up in Cleveland, Ohio. Ray contacted Jerome's friend Mitch, who knew of a plastic surgeon, in pursuit of his new identity.

Fr. Thom took great pains to follow the developments of his so called daughter's arrest and arraignment. He contacted the Diocese in Albany and made arrangements to have the daily newspaper delivered to him on a weekly basis, so that he could follow her trial.

The more Cindy thought about things, the more she thought her contact with Hector/Jerome had some relevance. She was scared of publicity, if Fr. Jerome should be exposed Cindy was of the opinion that Jerome would stop at nothing to avoid prison time. And Cindy wanted to keep her extortion out of the picture. But what if Jerome had something to do with Jas's death what if he hired a hit man who had killed Jas thinking it was me? Cindy was sure she should let her lawyer know about this incident with Jerome. Cindy concluded that the possibility existed that if Rob was telling the truth, a remote possibility existed that she was framed, or missed her date with death.

Jerome kept strong, hoped and prayed that no one could connect him to this murder. To some extent he felt safe due to his disguise and his distance away.

Cindy was becoming more convinced that she would like to speak to the old priest. Twenty years in prison would be more than a big break from her calls to the Diocese. Jerome would be happy that he will not have to deal with her for two decades.

But how can she begin to prove her innocence, with a public defender, and limited resources. She thought to herself that bad luck had followed her ever since she started to contact the Diocese. She felt pretty sure that she was convinced Rob had a hand in Jasmine's death, but knew she could not prove it.

Her lawyer had asked her about any unusual events or occurrences she could recall in the past six months to a year. Her brief encounter with Hector the private eye, whom she felt sure, was Jerome, was foremost in her thoughts. She almost started to speak then changed her mind. She thought she should withhold that strange encounter, for a little while longer. Then a dose of reality hit her, as she suddenly realized that pretty soon she would be on trial for her life. Cindy remembered that this was the second time she came under suspicion for murder.

The first time the investigations cleared her, but this time the prosecutor would try to make the charges stick. This was not the time or place to play Russian roulette with her life she decided that, come what may, she was going to let her lawyer know everything. Cindy waited patiently for her lawyer to return.

Jerome stumbled over his father's mail by chance. What really interested him was a number of Albany daily newspapers. He sat himself in his father's office and began to browse. He knew that those papers could shed some light on everything that had taken place recently, and help to clear up the confusing mess circulating in his head.

Since he was once again finding it difficult to contact his brother Ray, he wanted to know what was what. Most of what he was hoping to be reality was apparently a dream and most of what he now hoped to be a dream, was real.

The Death of Jasmine at Cindy's home was real; now in hindsight he wished her death was a dream. After the event, even a fool is wiser and Jerome wished he could take back now what he had done, especially since it was the wrong person who was killed. Had it been Cindy who was killed, he wondered would he be remorseful.

Jerome's own selfishness had overcome all logic, all the papal rules and more importantly, one of the ten commandments, "Thou shall not kill" meaning that it is wrong to kill another human being for any reason other than in self defense or in war.

Now Jerome became convinced that he dreamt of his father's death and burial, for his father was very much alive. The Albany newspapers made Jerome aware that the heist was real and not only was it a success. Jimmy was a prime suspect in what the police was now calling an inside job.

Little mention was made of Ray except that the police were looking for a fourth person whom they thought was the mastermind behind that robbery.

Finally, the status of Cindy's trial meant more to Jerome than ever. He wondered if, out of anger and revenge, he would be turned in by Cindy. It was not the prison time, he was worried about. His focus was on his pride and his position as a Priest being labeled a sex offender.

Now more than ever Fr. Jerome wanted no part to do with her trial, instead he thought he should encourage his father to help Cindy, under the pretense that since Cindy was his daughter, he should support her to the end. In fact ,Jerome thoughts were centered on self preservation.

He thought to himself that once Cindy knew they were supporting her financially she would keep her mouth shut about the past to everyone, so that the help and support would continue. Cindy needed all the help and support she could get.

Cindy on the other had no idea that her mother was alive let alone that she was applying pressure to Fr. Thom for Cindy to get a highly reputed attorney.

Fr. Thom was in the midst of figuring out how he would be able to get funds to pay for a top lawyer and how he could keep this whole matter a secret from the Church and media. Suddenly the phone rang; it was Ray on the line. Fr. Thom thought first it might have been Olga; he was relieved and happy to hear from his son for a change. He had no idea that Ray was the mastermind behind the heist he had read about in the Albany newspaper. He did not pay much attention to that story. Like Jerome he was preoccupied with Cindy's trial. Ray sounded upbeat and happy. He told his father he was in Las Vegas instead of where he really was and that he had come into a large sum of money from gaming. Fr. Thom was delighted to hear the good news.

Fr. Thom always preached against gambling but now the thought of his son winning a large sum of money provided Fr. Thom with hope he could look past the wrongs he preached about if his son could help him out of this predicament.

Fr. Thom was eager to find out how much money his son was talking about. At first the old priest purposely ignored mention of Ray's winnings and just asked Ray how he was doing and asked him about the problem he was having with the two thugs. He asked his son, that since he now had a large sum of money if it would be enough to take care of the problem he was having. It was Fr. Thom's way of finding out what this sum was.

Ray told his father it was much more than he could ever imagine and that he had already made his payment in the full, so he no longer had those guys after him. Ray was lying to his Father. He was not even going to repay the loan shark, as he led his dad to believe, because of the beatings he received from Scar and Marble.

Fr. Thom came to a point in the conversation that he could no longer contain his curiosity and the words came out before he could control himself, "How much did you win son"?

Ray told him his winnings were more than a million dollars.

After Jerome spoke with Ray briefly, Fr. Thom was surprised at his demeanor. He had seen Jerome in that frame of mind, only when it was time for his vacation. He appeared relaxed, calm and happy.

Fr. Thom much preferred to deal with his son when he was like this. He wanted his actions to be justified at least by his son. They spoke and Jerome expressed his agreement for his father to help Cindy get a high priced attorney. Jerome expressed his agreement; after all if Cindy is found guilty then he will not have to worry about further investigations. But with a smart attorney anything is possible yet if she is found not guilty the case may go cold for lack of evidence. After all is said and done there was no way to link me to the crime, Fr. Jerome thought.

This sudden change in Jerome's attitude made Fr. Thom happy that at least he did not have to fight to do what he wanted to do. Fr. Thom hadn't the vaguest idea the reason for his son's sudden change of mind. He did not have the slightest idea that Jerome's attitude stemmed from the fact that he was in bigger trouble than Fr. Thom could imagine. Jerome's future still hemmed on the outcome of Cindy's trial to some extent.

Ray was the mastermind behind the whole plot and exploited everyone around him. First, he used Kelly when he first arrived in Albany to find his way around. He used Jimmy for a place to stay, then it was Martha to plant drugs and money to frame the thugs which backfired. The thugs left before that plan could be implemented. Jimmy was now a suspect in the armored car heist. Ray made a mess of almost everyone he came in contact for the benefit of his hidden identity.

He convinced Fr. Jerome that a change of place and identity would better benefit Jerome's cause. The night before the heist Ray visited the Diocese using Jerome's old lady disguise. He then drugged Jerome's drink and left the Diocese dressed as a priest. That explained why Jerome was so incoherent and the reason for him sleeping as long as he did. As well as his elaborate dream of his father's demise.

He spent the night at Bob's home awaiting the heist knowing that Bob could not tell the difference between Ray and Jerome. Ray was taking every precaution; he was erasing his tracks in preparation for his new identity. He was not prepared to share the loot with anyone, not even his brother. Ray just wanted Jerome to be blamed if any trace could be made of the heist, in order to save himself. He also convinced Mary that her husband was involved with the mob, and that it was in her best interest if she left her husband and went with Ray, since her husband was heavy in debt to the mob and word had it the mob was closing in on him and she would suffer the same consequences with him. Ray was growing tired of his bachelor lifestyle and beginning to fall in love with Mary. He also thought she would be a good disguise for him and Ray was beginning to think that a change could be of benefit

Kelly was in prison doing six months for drug possession and prostitution, so far she was the only one to escape Ray's schemes she was in for her own doing.

Paul, Jimmy and John were victims of Ray's scheme

to get money, so he could change his identity. And what was to say, that Jerome and Martha would not soon follow. Jimmy for sure was in custody pending the outcome of the heist investigation.

Ray seemed to be bad news, to his colleagues. He was halfway truthful to Mary. He did not let her know that he was on the run from the two thugs, and pretty soon he might be on the FBI top ten wanted list.

Ray never told anyone that he was on the run because he had stolen a shipment of drugs single handed from the mob. Ray did not know that Scar and Marble's job was to inflict pain rather than kill him until he paid three times what the drugs were worth. Ray did not know that the street value of the drugs was worth over a million dollars, neither did he know there was a contract on his life. He did not even tell Mary or Jerome about the drugs he took and sold for below street value to get it off his hands quickly. Nor did he tell Mary he was on the run from the two thugs. Jerome of course knew about the thugs, Ray was pretty sure that by this time the thugs would be locked up for drug possession and armed robbery.

Mary didn't realize that Ray would soon be on the FBI top ten wanted list once Jimmy decided to implicate Ray, who Jimmy knew as James as the mastermind behind the armored car heist.

Once again he lied; Ray never borrowed money from a loan shark as he made his brother to believe. Instead the real reason the thugs were behind him was because of the drugs he stole that belonged to the mob. Ray knew that Jimmy would be the main target of the heist investigation, but would not crack or break under pressure once he knew the money was safe.

Ray was indeed a double crossing scheming crook, no wonder he was always on the run from someone. He was convinced that once Paul and John realized that they were set up, they would willingly sell him out.

He was hoping to be settled and stable in one place by that time, a place where he would have everything at his disposal and would not have to go outdoors more than necessary. His final goal was to leave the USA for Europe, Brazil, Mexico or the Caribbean. Due to all the plans Ray had formulated a change of identity would certainly be necessary.

Mary was beginning to admire Ray's brilliance and his desire. Being on the run so far with Ray, was exciting, intriguing and never dull. It was certainly better than that dull life in Massachusetts. Every day now seemed like an adventure. She was becoming more and more attached to Ray partly because he turned out to be more adventurous than Bob. Mary had spent the better part of her twenty year marriage to Bob taking care of their two children Bob Jr. and Jen. The highlight of her excitement would be a day at the ball park after Bob Jr. was old enough to play baseball or a trip with Jen to the mall when she was old enough to enjoy shopping. Apart from those events, the only other thing Mary could look forward to was vacation time and lately a visit from Jerome when her husband was away on his business trips. Mary hadn't the vaguest idea that what Ray had told her about her husband was really Ray's situation. Ray was now on the run, initially due to nonpayment to a Drug Debt.

She wished she had met Ray twenty five years ago. This was the very first time she had left home without her husband.

She decided that she had made a good decision to get away from Bob for as long as possible. So far she had no regrets and enjoyed this new exciting way of life. Mary knew that Ray was on the run but she enjoyed the excitement of the disguises being made to look different, the different make ups and attire she wore, and hopping from hotel to hotel.

This was by far better than sitting at home waiting on Bob to return in most cases, or the occasional phone call from her daughter and grand kids. They were away in Paris for a few months and now the phone calls would be routine, in any event her daughter would get the answering machine, if and when she called. Jen would most likely think that everything was okay. There would be no way for Bob to contact Mary. For one, they were not on speaking terms and secondly, Ray made her leave her cell phone at her home.

Ray let Mary know that they could be traced by the cell phone towers from city to city, county to county, state to state. In addition, if a person was really kidnapped, the kidnapped person would not take their cell phone with them.

If what Ray had said to her was true then she had every reason not to consider returning. Ray had told her how much he loved her. She never even afforded her husband of twenty five years the opportunity to respond to the allegation made by Ray, about Bob's debt to the mob. Mary did not even give matters a second thought; she was so tired of her husband's infidelity, she just took off blindly with Ray. Mary never looked back; she just looked forward for fun and excitement

The Deadly Priest

CHAPTER TWELVE

Cindy and Rob's trial was now just two weeks away when Jerome received yet another shock seeing Olga in church, in the front row. Olga made her presence not only seen but felt. Her visit to the church was an indication to Fr. Thom that she meant business.

Once again, Jerome was stunned by this latest development. He knew he was not dreaming now, but where had she been all this time?

Fr. Thom was visibly shaken, wanting to retreat into the vestry and not return. He felt dizzy but tried his best to maintain his balance and composure. It was difficult for him to concentrate on the sermon he was delivering. Eventually he rambled through the mass and was more than happy to reach the end. Fr. Jerome was also having a difficult time delivering communion. He made several mistakes which he attempted to cover up and make look normal.

It was time for confession and guess who was among the first in the confession box. Olga.

Fr. Thom could hardly keep his composure; he did not want Fr. Jerome to take her confession. Fr. Thom suddenly flipped the script and decided that he would replace his son in the confessional.

Jerome was enraged but had no choice but to control his anger. What Jerome did not know was that his father wanted to speak to Olga in his office, this time with Jerome present for his help and support.

Fr. Thom took Olga's confession pretending that she needed counseling and led her to his office.

Fr. Jerome hurried through the rest of the confessions then proceeded straight to his father's office. He met Olga and his father having coffee over a normal conversation.

Jerome greeted Olga with a hug then went through the formalities. Then he got right down to the business at hand, "Where have you been all this time?" he asked. Olga did not try to hide the fact that she was incarcerated on armed robbery charges for five years. She wanted to come clean so that the two priests would not have anything on her. She confessed that her action stemmed from her crack addiction. She was the getaway driver of a botched robbery of an overnight deli.

Olga explained that her time in prison had awakened her awareness, that she was traveling on the wrong road and that she vowed never to use any drugs as long as she lived. Olga indicated that she was clean for the five years of incarceration and since being released and for the past three weeks to a month, she has been drug free on the outside. Her husband Nathaniel, the other accomplice in the robbery, was doing fifteen to life since this was his third strike.

Olga said that she did not let Cindy know where she

and her husband were for the duration of her incarceration, but now that she was finally free, she would discuss her absence with her daughter if, and when, Cindy was released from custody.

Despite doing five years in the penitentiary Olga looked and appeared upbeat. She sounded like she had just discovered how important her freedom was and how depressing her crack addiction was. Olga was proud of her achievements in prison and the fact that she had finally completed her GED.

Jerome could not contain his curiosity any longer even though he knew the nature of her visit. "So where do you live now and what brings you to Massachusetts?" was his next question, Jerome was the one conducting the interview. Olga replied, "Well Jerome, I was incarcerated there because the crime was committed in Albany but I am currently in Massachusetts visiting a relative. But thank God, I did all my time. As a result I am not on parole and can be by my daughter's side when her trial begins in two weeks."

She lied, she was on parole without electronic monitoring.

"My reason for being here at the church today is to plead with Fr. Thom to assist his daughter to get a proper attorney. A public defender is not the lawyer you want to represent you in a first degree murder charge. Do not get me wrong, there are very good public defenders out there who sometimes work hard, but there is always a limit to what the state will pay for in terms of research and that is why I say it the way I do."

Before Jerome could say a word, Olga continued, her crack head instincts of sympathy seeking kicking in. "I know that in the past we reached a settlement and that my addiction got the better of the funds, but I can assure you all, this will be the last favor."

"Did I hear you say 'his daughter'?" Jerome asked incredibly.

"My dear son, you were too young to accept or understand. I conceived Cindy while my husband was incarcerated and your father was the only man I had a relationship with while he was in prison. Fortunately, my husband and I had conjugal visits but I am sure that Cindy belongs to your father. He has also agreed that Cindy is his child. Had it not been for his elected position and had he not reentered the church scene, he would openly admit it, especially since your mother is no longer alive."

Jerome was stunned. This was not something that he was hearing for the first time. Hearing it from Olga really blew Jerome's mind especially when Olga referred to his deceased mother. Jerome was about to explode. He was really having a hard time trying to keep calm.

Father Thom knew his son was angry so he stepped in to try and change the conversation. "Olga, I would still be happy if we could do a DNA test to make sure. I am a priest and I should know the truth. I am not trying to deny that we did have a relationship but I will need to know for sure if I am her father or not."

Jerome got his chance. He always wanted to confront Olga about being set up for the purpose of keeping their skeletons in the closet. "So the plot was for you to put Cindy up to have sex with me so that the church paid what was thought to be compensation for the wrong I did to her. Although, you both knew that it was compensation to you, Olga, so you can keep this whole mess a secret. Now look what has happened to you. If you had gotten ten million from the settlement, the outcome of your life would be the same. You had to be stopped because you didn't seem to realize you were headed for prison time or death. I am happy that you have decided to turn your life around but who will clean up the mess I am in. Then again, as if you did not do enough damage, you are back to your ATM machine for more cash."

Olga knew she had Fr. Thom in the palm of her hand. She would stop at nothing to achieve her goal. Since she knew she had Fr. Thom cornered, ignoring Fr. Jerome totally, Olga continued, "How can we do a DNA test without alerting the media's attention to this situation?" she questioned.

Olga laid her cards on the table, "I understand how you feel Jerome, but you have to realize that right now your set up theory is completely unfounded and the fact of the matter is you were caught having sex with a minor which you admitted. Fortunately, your father has succeeded in keeping it from the Attorney General's attention. This situation should have already been reported. However, need I remind you that the statute of limitations makes it current. Now you guys have but one choice, get Cindy a lawyer or I expose Fr. Thom's infidelity. He loses his position. Then I report your conduct to the attorney general. THIS SITUATION IS NOT UP FOR DISCUSSION, YOU DO WHAT I SAY, OR ELSE!"

Both father and son were at a loss for words. Stunned, shocked, dumbfounded, angry and outraged, would be good words to describe what was going through the minds of these two priests.

Jerome knew all along his hands were tied, now what would his next move be. He walked out of the meeting dazed.

Fr. Thom assured Olga that they would give her new demands some serious thought and he would have an answer in three to five days. Olga was confident and happy she had driven her point home to both men. Olga strutted out of the Diocese with her head held high.

The trial of John and Paul was also about to begin. The police were no closer to finding who the mastermind was, let alone begin looking for him, but Ray was covering his tracks especially because of the two thugs. He kept abreast with the news in Albany and New York City via satellite radio and he found out so far that the two robbers were not talking to the police or FBI. Ray knew that it would be quite some time before he had to worry about them. It was also being rumored around town that Jimmy was going to be charged as a co-conspirator.

One week later, the two armored car robbers pleaded guilty and sentencing was put off for three months to give investigators time to get the mastermind. The feds still could not figure out the central figure. Word was the two disciples, as they were called, would be sentenced to fifteen years to life. The feds were still hoping the robbers would give up the mastermind for a reduced sentence.

Jimmy was indeed charged as a co-conspirator in the robbery, he was also charged with identity theft. He hired a high priced attorney and, at his arraignment, pleaded not guilty to all charges. He knew that the DA could not link him to the two robbers. There was a strong possibility that he would receive a plea deal which would result in the identity theft charge being dropped, if he could give information that would lead to the capture and conviction of the mastermind, James, as he was now known.

They did not have any evidence that Jimmy had participated in the crime. That was just a theory. The two thugs were questioned at length about their whereabouts in Albany and released once it was clear they did not know James, John or Jimmy. They did not tell the investigators that they were looking for Ray.

The investigations revealed that they were on a plane to New York at the time of the robbery. The cops never had enough to link the two thugs with a crime, even though they were suspicious that it would be a big coincidence if they were not there to plan the robbery of the armored car. It seemed very suspicious that they did not have anything to do with that heist. It was hard to believe.

The two thugs now vowed to get Ray at all costs due to the inconvenience brought about by their visit to Albany in search of him. This time he would not live to tell a tale. The thugs remained under police surveillance for the next three months making it difficult for them to do their work effectively.

Scar and Marble were one hundred percent sure that

Ray was involved with the planning of the heist. But since they wanted Ray so badly, they would not as much as whisper his name to the police. They wanted him for themselves.

Ray was feeling lucky. His initial plan was to head to Las Vegas with Mary once he got his new identity. He had faked Mary's kidnap, left Bob a ransom note for one million dollars in used notes.

He dyed her hair black and they were on their way. Ray stopped from time to time to call Bob from a pay phone with instructions on where and when to drop off the ransom so that the kidnapping would seem real.

Bob was cooperating with the kidnapper's request so he did not inform the cops of his wife's kidnapping for the first forty-eight hours, giving Ray the head start he so badly needed. Bob felt uncertain of being able to carry out the kidnapper's demand. He had a feeling that he was incapable of doing this on his own without the assistance of the police, so he finally got them involved.

Bob gave a complete description of what he thought she was wearing along with recent photographs of his wife. By the fourth day, Ray no longer thought it necessary to further torment Bob so he didn't even bother to call in further demands since he knew that calling would be an easy way for the authorities to track him down. Due to Bob's action of not notifying the authorities immediately and the fact that there were no calls since he alerted police he was now being looked at as a suspect in the disappearance of his wife. A massive search ensued but Mary was nowhere to be found. The church and local authorities searched in and around the neighborhood for new dug-up dirt. Bob was outraged to be considered as a suspect but the police dared not lay a hand on him due to his financial status, and the influence he had in Lowell.

But now, Bob would be segregated, tried and be found guilty in the eyes of the public. Whatever happened to innocent until proven guilty? The police did not even have evidence of foul play or a crime. They searched Bob and Mary's residence and came up empty handed which was obvious since Mary was not killed. It was a case where her kidnap was a fake so there would be no crime scene. It would be considered a missing person until a body could be found.

Ray was careful, whenever they stopped, to always let Mary stay apart from where he stayed. Ray took great pains to register in separate rooms. He wasn't even aware that no one, as yet, had connected him to the heist, not even the FBI.

Ray would often change from Greyhound to Amtrak to an occasional stolen vehicle. He avoided the use of credit cards and when driving always remained within the speed limits. It took Ray less than two days to arrive in Cleveland, Ohio. Ray had no problem finding Mitch, nicknamed Foggy. They sat down and reminisced about old times back in the days stuff.

Their recollections brought them tons of laughter, and then eventually it was time to get down to business. Foggy knew that Ray was not there for a social call. Foggy contacted a plastic surgeon to make Ray look different and ten years older. Foggy also had driver's license and credit cards made out for Ray in the name of Henry Bertog, a homeless crack addict. Now Ray was free to use the electronic method of payment if he chose to do so. The three hour procedure to transform him to Henry went well. The only set back was that now he would have to be seen by the surgeon for at least six months.

All together, Ray spent roughly two hundred on documents and fifty thousand on surgery to look like Henry Bertog. But now it was well worth it.

Also, included in the money spent, was a little alteration to make Mary look different. She would be Sylvia Bertog. Foggy provided them with fake documents, SS cards, driver's license, birth and marriage certificates the whole nine yards.

Ray grew restless after a few months and took off to Vegas. He promised to return for his follow-up with his plastic surgeon, a convicted rapist who could no longer practiced surgery legally in the United States. His license was revoked after he was found guilty of raping one of his clients while she was sedated. The surgeon claimed it was consensual sex but was found guilty. He met Foggy while doing his three years in the pen. He now worked for people in Ray's situation, close friends and relatives, and on rare occasions, the Mob. The money was always great because Dr. Woodsen customers were willing to pay whatever the surgeon charged. The money was tax free. This was how Dr. Woodsen made a living - a very lucrative living.

The trials of Cindy and Rob were due to start in less than two weeks. Cindy had her high priced attorney, Mr. Francis Mentz Esq., a successful criminal defense lawyer. Fr. Thom was in luck because he and Francis had attended school in Massachusetts up through high school. They hung out together as kids, and got into trouble together. They also played football and baseball prior to attending college. The two stayed in touch with each other throughout the years and visited, mostly on holidays, especially Christmas and Thanksgiving. On more than one occasion, the two families went on vacation together.

Francis also attended Fr. Thom's wife, Esther's, funeral.

Mr. Mentz agreed to represent Cindy for expenses; he was not going to receive any other payment. He decided to represent Cindy because he knew the background circumstances of Olga and Cindy's birth. Fr. Thom seemed convinced, at the time of her birth, he was her father and no doubt had innocently convinced his friend to that effect.

Meanwhile, Fr. Thom was taking no chances of being linked to the trial of Cindy due to everything that took place between her and the Diocese. He wanted to keep the incident between Jerome and Cindy away from the media and, obviously, from the trial.

Despite being close friends, Fr. Thom visited Francis under the pretense of the church. The two men agreed that Mr. Mentz would be paid at the conclusion of the trial.

Mr. Mentz got to work immediately and filed motions to have the trial moved to another jurisdiction as well as to have separate trials for the two defendants. All motions were heard and turned down. This was a strategy Francis used a lot because eventually the judge feels obligated to grant a motion or two in his favor later on in the trial. In some cases the latter decision could make a major change in the trial.

Ray, on the other hand, was also laying the ground work for Fr. Jerome to be the main suspect in the disappearance of Mary. The police were sure they were on the trail of a major kidnapping.

Ray was shocked to eventually find out that the two thugs were now in Summerset, Massachusetts, obviously in search of him. Ray had things figured out a lot different than how they occurred. He could not figure that Martha, for some reason, did not carry out her part of the deal. He also could not figure out that Scar Face and Marble Eye were still on the loose in Massachusetts. Nor did Ray ever consider they had offered Martha five thousand for her help to get rid of the thugs, but were giving her ten thousand dollars to plant drugs in the thug's room. It seems they never realized that they did not even give her any money prior to the ten thousand in cash. Somehow, Martha was aware that ten was better than the five thousand they had promised her. Martha knew that a promise is comfort for a fool and a bird in the cage is worth ten in the bush.

It appears quite obvious why Martha took everything for herself, Ray's guess was that she knew that they could not go to the cops and in so doing, left the thugs running free and Ray would have a major headache once he found out. He hadn't the slightest idea what was going on. Ray just felt pretty sure Martha had taken care of business on his behalf without even receiving a cash advance. Where was the money to pay her coming from? No one had the slightest idea where Ray or the money was at this time.

The other robbers wanted to cooperate with the Feds for a lesser sentence. They knew they were looking at a long time behind bars. The thought of long hard time made many tough hard core criminals soften up and become star witnesses for the prosecution in exchange for a lesser sentence. At this point in time, they had nothing to lose than a few extra years in the pen. Based on the information they received, it became quite obvious that they were set up. They wanted to remain defiant of the pressure the Feds would try to enforce. On the other hand, the two individuals knew they were taken for a ride and screwed in the process. Revenge was obvious, but they knew very well that the prison population never likes rats. But in this case, the situation was different. Holding out on the Feds would mean holding on to long sentence time.

To Paul and John, a plea deal looked like their best deal. Since their arrest, they were never allowed to see each other, let alone communicate. What would be their next move? They were housed in two different jails, ten miles apart. Paul was indignant at the thought of how naive and vulnerable Ray had made them to be for his own personal gains. It seemed likely that they did not need an orchestra in order to sing, yet both men seemed bent on remaining quiet. They both kept their traps shut despite their circumstances. The two disciples never uttered a word.

The robbery squad theory was an inside job however, they were puzzled to find out how and where the remainder of the cash went. For those answers they turned to Jimmy who was now considered the master mind of this robbery. The newspapers captioned "inside job" says the Feds and "highway robbery". The Feds background check on Jimmy also revealed that he had lied on his application, stating that he had a clean criminal background. Now the Feds were zeroing in on those facts and the reality of the situation was making Jimmy very uncomfortable. Since the heist Jimmy was held in custody. The longer the investigation progressed, the less likely it seemed that Jimmy would be released. In other words the cops had no reason to believe his story.

In the meantime, Ray made his escape via Cleveland, Ohio for two reasons. One, Foggy his friend now managed a successful air charter company. Ray was banking on his friend of many years to put him on a reliable private air charter to just about anywhere in the world he needed to go. His first aim was Las Vegas and eventually in the hills and desert of Phoenix, Arizona. He had only seen that way of life briefly in passing while being on the run from Scar Face and Marble Eye. He became impressed with the people Hemet's way of life but he never stopped long enough to find out their source of survival. All he knew was what he was told, that they were a hate group who disliked the federal government because they were forced to pay income tax, which they now totally refused to pay. He felt pretty sure he would be welcomed with a large contribution compliments of the FDIC. He was confident that would give him some cover until things blew over.

Ray was no fool. His intention was never to let his guard down and tell anyone the truth of his past for fear he would be turned in for a sizable ransom. So, he thought to himself, he would keep his past under wraps.

The second reason he made Ohio his choice for escape and disguise, was that his friend could be called an expert in disguises. He did actually spend three years as a makeup artist in Hollywood. He was doing fine until he started forging his director's signature. He was eventually indicted on forgery resulting in grand theft of almost a quarter of a million dollars for which he was convicted and sentenced to five years in prison.

Foggy, as he was called, was also an expert at forging documents, and in this day of identity theft, he could probably make an easy fortune. Yet he chose to get married and raise a family. His son was now three years old and his daughter was expected in two to three months. Foggy decided jail was not where he wanted to be. These days, he devoted his time and energy to the charter service as a front, but now only worked for close friends and relatives. This way he could be more selective and minimize the risk of being caught. It was rumored that, while Foggy was incarcerated, the warden had strict instructions that

Foggy never go near the library except on a one on one basis, supervised so that the person supervising him could have undivided attention at all times to what he was doing.

Once Foggy made an identical pass to the ones used for prisoner's release, from the computer in the library. He once pulled that stunt while being held in a minimum security prison in Arizona. He almost made it to freedom except for one alert prison guard who knew he was not scheduled for release. The guard double checked with the warden. The warden had a hard time determining his signature against the forgery on the release form. They both looked authentic. Foggy had to be out for the signing of a multi million deal. Foggy was supposed to forge all the signatures on that contract worth over one hundred million dollars. He would have been all the signatures on that contract.

Foggy made money in his short stint at college forging papers and professors signatures. He knew he could make money without a college education. He was street wise. Ray was thankful he knew Foggy well so he decided to stay for a few days, until Foggy could have things arranged. His intention, no doubt, was to charter a private jet the rest of the way. Everything was going according to plan.

The Cindy and Rob trial was set to start in one week's time. The defense leaked to the media they had a witness who would testify he saw an old lady leave Cindy's apartment complex around the time the murder occurred. And that this same witness would be prepared to testify that the person seemed surprisingly tall for their apparent age. The defense team was scoring heavy media pre trial theory. On the other hand, the prosecution was demanding a polygraph test which the defense vehemently refused. This trial was headed for legal fireworks with two of the best lawyers in the business going head to head against each other. Cindy's new lawyer was paid for by an anonymous person or persons who were sure she was innocent. Fr. Thom and/or Jerome come to mind. Cindy appeared dazed, drugged or depressed, one can safely say in a world of her own. Perhaps wishing and hoping for this nightmare to end, her new lawyer Mr. Mendez seemed confident he could exonerate her. He seemed to believe in her innocence.,

Jerome was more than curious to find out who the witness could be, and what he or she had to say. In the meantime Scar Face and Marble Eye decided to pay Jerome a visit at the nine am mass. Jerome had assumed his active duty and delivered mass on that Sunday.

Jerome kept abreast of the pre-trial reports in Albany but much could not be said because the prosecution had won a motion to suppress. That meant that Jerome could no longer follow the developments of the trial since nothing more of substance could be said to the media until the trial got started.

All at once Jerome knew that the present situation warranted him to get out of the Diocese so he could have firsthand knowledge of what was taking place with the trial. He also reasoned, within himself, that it was time he took care of Scar Face and Marble Eye once and for all. He had to take care of business because those thugs were on to him and words could not convince them he was not Ray. The deadly priest decided that his best defense was going to be offense. He did it once and he was damned sure going to have to do it again. On second thought, he was going to lure them to him.

Jerome got busy calling all the nearby motels and car rental agencies until he could pretty well narrow down where the two thugs were staying. His amateur detective work paid off and Jerome, disguised as the little old lady, paid the thugs a visit in their motel room. By this time Jerome had become a pro at his disguise.

He used the old lady disguise to leave the Diocese then he registered as a priest at Motel Luxury as it was called. Jerome once again could not even try to piece together the sudden twists and turns his life had suddenly taken.

First it was Cindy's allegation of rape then thanks to her mother and Fr. Thom they resolved a settlement. Then just when Jerome thought everything was okay, Cindy comes along but this time for even more money than she had. That's what a blackmailer does. Then comes Ray at what seemed to Jerome to be the best time to be Jerome's brother, small time hoodlum Jerome had all the confidence that Ray would carry out his dirty work. To Jerome's dismay, murder seemed the last thing Ray would do. The deadly priest knew the only way to put an end to blackmail was to get rid of the blackmailer permanently. But now she was in custody.

The Deadly Priest

This was not the way he had planned things. He thought he had seen the last of Cindy but he killed her friend instead. Now he was eager to find out if the truth would come out that it was someone other than Cindy who had killed Jasmine. Instead Jerome found himself in a bigger ditch than when he first started out. Fr. Jerome soon found out what Ray was saying was the truth. You rob a bank and you may get away free. But you kill and the cops will hunt you to the bitter end, because there is no statute of limitations where murder is concerned. Then, as if he didn't have enough problems of his own, along comes the two thugs. Hearing his brother's account of what he could remember, Jerome was surely not eager to meet them face to face. He was tormented to think for a while what type of priest would want to see his father dead, was it wrong to give forgiveness, to have compassion?

Jerome wanted badly to call a senior priest and go to confession. Yet he knew the nature of his confession would land him in prison, maybe for the rest of his life.

The preliminary hearing into the death of Cindy's friend Jasmine began without the expected fireworks. Or maybe it fell short of the media frenzy/expectation. The defense and prosecution seemed a lot more civil than was anticipated until the drifter theory came up. The prosecution would try anything they could. The defense tried to play things calm but the prosecution was not having it. The prosecution seemed to let everything slide, asking minimal questions, from the detective in charge of the investigation, with the hope that the defense would leave that theory alone. With the hope the defense did not or could not find that witness, the defense took the opportunity to question the detective in charge of the investigation at length to see what was the strength of their case.

AFTER JURY SELECTION

===============================

OPENING STATEMENTS BEGIN!

=======================================

THE DEFENSE ATTORNEY STARTED!

"My client is not a murderer she was planning a night out on the town with Jasmine who by this time had become her best friend. Those two women were planning to have a good time at some nightclub then return safely to their respective homes. If the plan was to kill Jasmine why would anyone let it happen in their home so that they could be fingered as a suspect?

"The defense intends to prove my client innocent based on facts not on any technicality. Ladies and gentlemen of the jury when all the facts of this case are heard you will have no other verdict than not guilty of all charges."

Cindy felt a little better after Mr. Mentz opening statement.

Scar and Marble were desperate to pick up Ray's trail, seems that they were really doing a great job of following Ray's trail, only problem was Ray always kept a step ahead of them. Ray found comfort in his new disguise. He felt comfortable that he would not be easily identified by those thugs. Now that he had his new appearance.

His experience with them was so traumatic that Ray was not even trying if possible to be in the same state as those thugs no time soon maybe ever. That would be the extent of how scared Ray was of the beating he suffered at their hands.

Scar and Marble were now in Summerset, Massachusetts desperately looking for Ray due to the humiliation at being arrested and questioned for something they had no knowledge of, they were determined to punish Ray, to the point of torture near death. Even though they were not aware that Ray was involved with the heist their presence in Albany was in search of Ray. Had he not been in Albany they would not have been in search of him there and would never be suspected of the heist.

They were very angry now to the point that they were now using their own funds towards travel expenses hoping to find Ray. The two thugs now took the search for Ray personal and would stop at nothing to find Ray. They were going to leave no stone unturned.

After six or seven days in Massachusetts they found Bob the millionaire pilot who told them about Fr. Jerome at the Diocese. They really did not have to do anything to Bob because now that his wife was MIA he was hearing rumors of his wife's infidelity with Jerome while he was away on his regular business trips. Bob somehow began to suspect that Jerome had something to do with his wife sudden disappearance.

But had no proof, he was more than happy when the two thugs came by to direct them to the Diocese, as if the two troubled priests did not have enough on their hands.

Bob knew that those two guys were dangerous but at this time Bob was after any form of revenge, for what Fr. Jerome had done.

Bob these days was disgraced in more ways than one. First he was now considered a suspect in the disappearance of his wife, then added to that he now knew that Mary was having an affair with Jerome while he was on his business trips, but for the most part while he was spending time with Laura in Albany.

Since Mary's apparent kidnapping, Bob did not attend Church and the community was divided at what had happened to Mary, some people thought Bob had something to do with it, while others thought he was completely innocent of all allegations.

Bob was never charged due to his millionaire status, and secondly due to lack of evidence of a crime.

The thugs were happy with the information Bob supplied them. They quizzed Bob about Ray having a twin because they wanted to make certain Ray had not faked his way into the church, as a priest as part of his disguise. But it became clear to Scar and Marble that Bob had known both Jerome and Ray all their life. So the thugs were convinced that the person who they thought to be Ray was really his brother and decided that the next day being Sunday they would be happy to attend Mass and possible confession. They promised Bob that they would get the information from Jerome of the whereabouts of Ray as well as his wife. They said it as though Jerome knew Ray and Mary's whereabouts but no one connected Ray and Mary as being together. Jerome was holding the brunt of the blame, for Mary's disappearance.

At least in the mind of Bob at this time, Bob was optimistic that he would get news of Mary from the two thugs because he could tell that those guys were mean and was definitely in no mood to play games. Given their own situation, their false arrest and questioning for the heist in Albany, it seems that they were ready to hurt someone or anyone, priest or nun if they had to in order to gain the information they needed.

The following day Scar and Marble paid a visit to the Diocese.

The trial of Rob and Cindy had entered its sixth week and the prosecution case was coming to an end without much surprises. Prior to the start of this trial the defense team had indicated they had information that a tall old lady was seen leaving Cindy's apartment following the sound of two shots being fired but most people thought it to be fire crackers.

Mr. Nelson the DA was adamant that the defense was still holding on to the drifter theory. Mr. Nelson knew that he did not have a strong case and the drifter theory which both defense attorneys made mention could create questions in the minds of the jury. Mr. Nelson knew that once the drifter theory came into play as evidence, he would not be able to convince the jury beyond reasonable doubt.

Mr. Nelson was running for re-election and only for that reason did he bring these two defendants to trial. Usually a case of this nature with insufficient evidence would not be brought before the court, but the DA was hoping for more evidence before this case could come to an end. Mr. Nelson's game plan would be to suppress any new evidence that the defense should come up with. This new development was certainly not in his favor. This was not the type of new information he was looking out for. Now it seemed he was running out of options reflected an air of anger and lost confidence. Both Cindy and her attorney seemed happy to see Mr. Nelson upset for a change. Cindy was convinced Mr. Mentz was doing the best he could for her.

The defense team investigator was close to locating the witness who saw the tall blonde old lady leave Cindy's home and the defense was asking the judge for three days before the start of their case. Notwithstanding the judge should rule against that motion, Mentz's strategy would be to let Mr. Cottrell examine the witnesses he had for an extended time. For instance, they would recall the ballistics expert and play for time, because due to the fact that all he had was the type of the gun and the caliber of the bullet but was unable to connect either Rob or Cindy to the gun.

In an unprecedented move by the judge, he granted Mr. Mentz motion to adjourn the trial for seventy two hours to give the defense time to present their case.

Mr. Mentz plan worked just like it always did, a

number of motions turned down, then eventually a major decision in Mr. Mentz's favor. Things were looking good for the defense.

Mr. Nelson exploded; he immediately informed the judge that he was working on an appeal of his decision in the State court of appeal to be heard by a circuit judge the following day. Mr. Nelson's appeal would be heard at seven am so as not to affect the progress of the trial which usually starts at nine am. If the appeal went in the prosecution favor then the trial would resume at nine am.

All of a sudden this quiet trial, despite being high profile due to the presence of Mr. Mentz, had erupted into the usual courtroom theatrics Mentz was known to bring to a trial. The trial that was losing interest to the media was now headed to be a big courtroom battle.

Mr. Nelson's appeal was denied.

When court resumed the courtroom was once again packed with reporters the prosecution was also filing a motion to suppress any additional witness brought at the end of the prosecution's case except the witness would submit to a polygraph test.

Mr. Mentz was on his feet like an explosion, Honorable Judge when I last checked, a polygraph test is inadmissible in a court of law and secondly the police cannot demand a defense witness take a polygraph test, that is unprecedented and if a precedence like this is created, then all witnesses will be subject to polygraph tests. All of a sudden this trial was headed for legal fireworks.

Judge Connolly summoned the three attorneys to a side bar conference. He said to the three attorneys that the two defendants were on trial for their lives and that it was the responsibility of the attorneys to present any evidence that would bring out the truth to ensure a fair trial. The judge explained that should the defense have a credible witness that could shed light on circumstances surrounding the truth he would be more than happy to hear that witness and would allow the witness to testify at this stage, without a lie detector test since as Mr. Mentz quite rightly said, it was unusual to have a witness take a lie detector test prior to giving testimony.

The judge went on to say that a lie detector test is still inadmissible and is mostly done to suspects not witnesses. Marble and Scar decided to pay Jerome a visit at the nine am mass, despite the fact that Jerome might not have the information they were looking forward to hearing.

By this time, Fr. Jerome had assumed his active duties and delivered mass on that Sunday.

The two thugs were convinced that Ray's days of running would soon be over once they could get their hands on Jerome, priest or no priest. They were convinced that they would torture Fr. Jerome to get the information they needed.

The thugs were also convinced Ray might be hiding somewhere in the Parish. They were still not aware that Ray was the mastermind behind the robbery of the armored truck they weren't even sure he had anything to do with the robbery that took place the same day they left Albany for New York.

The information the police had, was that the robbery was an inside job. It was possible a third person or persons were involved. This is what the thugs were able to gather based on the questioning by the police in New York City. The police questioned the thugs to rule out their participation in that heist.

At first they were convinced that since he was an identical twin, Jerome could be Ray, and Ray could be Jerome. It was becoming obvious that an attack would be imminent. Jerome appeared to them like a bird in a cage within reach of a cat. Even a pet cat would attack that bird if left alone. That is a natural instinct of the cats. Now the two thugs were in reach of Jerome. If he was really Ray at some point it appears he seemed to ignore them, if he was Ray he seemed as if he was the righteous harmless priest he was pretending to be, the thugs could not accept the fact that Jerome was not Ray.

Usually the thugs had no regards for family members. If they couldn't find the person they were looking for, they would torture or hurt the relatives that were available.

Jerome was not happy to see them because he hated those two guys desperately. Jerome could care less about them and he was prepared to take them on single handedly; he still had the gun that he accidentally killed Jasmine with. These days Jerome had too much rage and pent up anger. He was a ticking time bomb waiting to explode.

On the other hand the two thugs thought they would just hand to Jerome what was due to Ray.

Jerome knew that the two strange men could be the

thugs based on Ray's description. He knew that they were still after his brother, they came up for communion and Jerome muttered under his breath "kindly" await me in the confession box. The two nodded ok. Jerome did not know if he was doing the right thing or not.

Jerome did not know what to say to the thugs so he decided he was going to let the thugs begin the dialogue. He finished handing out communion then walked around to the vestry in an attempt to keep calm before going to the confession box. Jerome retrieved his gun which was coincidently hidden in the vestry. Jerome knew the violent nature of these goons, and he was going to take no chances with them.

Next he decided that he would follow the opening lines of the confession. A few minutes later Jerome was staring Marble Eye, face to face. He tried not to show his nervousness or fear. Jerome acted normal in an attempt to create some doubt within their minds even if they thought he was Ray.

Marble did not give Jerome a chance to say anything his first words were you can run but you cannot hide what make you think you were going to get away from us?

Jerome reply was "may God bless and keep you safely and sin no more" the dialogue with Scar went similarly. Jerome repeated his papal lines while Scar Face was in mid sentence. Jerome was not trying to hear what those thugs had to say and it appeared that they thought he was Ray anyway. Jerome did not know they had spoken to Bob who explained that he was not Ray. Now Fr. Jerome decided, brother or no brother, they were going to come after him and he had no other choice than to defend himself.

It became quite obvious; he needed time to sort things out.

The two thugs left the church without incident but that would only be the beginning of things to come. Jerome now kept his gun under his robe and his plan was to have it close by twenty four-seven because he knew they thought he was Ray and Jerome knew they would return to the Diocese at some point in time.

The following day Jerome contacted his father with a suggestion: and the suggestion was for him to go to Albany for a few days to oversee the trial of Cindy and at the same time give her and Olga moral support.

Jerome's only motive was to get away for a while from those thugs. Fr. Thom really did not like that idea because he did not want to risk the attention being brought to the Diocese. He knew the media would stop at nothing to find out their interest in the trial.

Jerome on the other hand was not going to the trial but rather he would be out in search of his brother instead. Jerome's plan was to visit his friend Foggy in Ohio to get away from the thugs for a while.

Fr. Thom told Jerome that was really not a good idea. Jerome insisted that he would like a few days to find his brother. Jerome did not let his father know about the thugs. Before their little impromptu meeting

The Deadly Priest

could be over the two thugs called to arrange another confession meeting which they said was urgent and could not wait for Sunday. Jerome knew what he was up against but was happy they had spoken to his father now instead of Jerome.

A confession appointment was scheduled for seven p.m. on the following day Monday. Jerome knew that for some reason he could not let those guys back into the church with his father taking their confession. He knew they were not there to confess. Jerome formulated a plan for their second encounter. He would be the security guard at the gate disguised of course.

Cindy's trial was soon coming to an end. Despite the seventy-two hour recess the defense still could not locate this mysterious witness who it was feared could shed light on the tall old lady that was seen in the area on the night of the murder.

Mr. Mentz had a little apprehension to that move in the beginning because he knew that if, at the end of the recess the defense came up empty handed, the move would backfire in the prosecution favor. Mr. Nelson came to court with an air of confidence because he was aware that the defense was returning to court empty handed and he could now use the recess to the jury as a stall for time.

Immediately at the resumption of the trial, Mr. Mentz addressed the judge. He let the judge know that they were unable to locate his witness despite strong leads the last good information they heard about the witness was that he was a retired trucker and had gone out of state with a fellow trucker. Mr. Mentz apologized to the court for this delay but assured the judge and jury efforts were still continuing to contact this witness and it was hoped that this witness could be located before the end of the trial.

Mr. Nelson was so happy that no witness was found, it was as though he held a permanent smirk throughout the remainder of the day.

The two thugs arrived thirty minutes before their scheduled time of confession. Little did they know they were not headed to a church they were headed to a WAR ZONE.

They were ambushed at gun point by the security guard before they could draw their guns. Jerome was in the back seat and was instructing them to drive to a secluded area. For a moment Scar looked like he wanted to retaliate but Marble told him not to. Jerome was behind them both in the back seat and he had his gun to the driver's head Marble was the driver.

Jerome made them give up their weapons one at a time, he unloaded the guns then dropped them in the car park, and then he told Marble to drive to a secluded area.

Jerome did not know what his next move would be but he knew those two guy were dangerous and it might be better for him to hurt them rather than them to hurt him.

Jerome wanted revenge for his twin brother. Now he

had an idea he would pistol whip them and let the car go over a ravine while they were unconscious to make things look like an accident. But just in case things should not go according to plan, Jerome wanted them to know he was not Ray as if that would make a difference especially after this encounter.

"My dear friends, or foe if you prefer to be called, I really wish to let you know that I am an identical twin I am well aware of the hurt and pain you inflicted on my brother, despite him telling you that he had the funds available to repay the loan shark. You did your illegal enforcement. You guys took it personal and hurt my brother to the point of near death, I would like you to know that when he hurt I hurt and most twins have what is called ESP Extra Sensory Perception. By that I mean I had strong feelings that something was going wrong with my brother. Had I not insisted to the NYPD that I thought my brother was in danger, he would have died for lack of medical attention.

"If that was the case the situation would be very much like it is here and now but the only difference was that I was going to be the one hunting you down."

Scar and Marble were so upset, they were not saying a word. They let him talk while they looked for an opportunity to get out of this situation.

"But now," Fr. Jerome continued, "thank God my prayers were answered and my twin brother is still alive. By the way guys what brings you to Massachusetts? And I need an answer. In search of Ray, I guess if I tell you he is not here will you go away, I am sure you will not, you are here to inflict hurt and pain on me, now that you have found out his brother lives here. I know you will stop at nothing once you got the upper hand, unfortunately the ball is in my court so don't look at me as a priest, the bible says to turn your other cheek.

"Meaning forgiveness, imagine turning the other cheek to you then I would certainly end up with a broken jaw." Jerome kept on talking venting his feelings to the two men that almost killed his brother. In between talking and giving driving instructions to Marble, example turn right, turn left etc.

In the meantime the two thugs were thinking of a way to disarm Jerome. Marble, the driver, was following his instructions. It was not the first time they were in a situation like the one they were in. This situation brought them back to the past.

Marble and Scar were Vietnam veterans. Marble a marine and Scar an army veteran. They both served in Vietnam. In addition, Marble was a disgraced ex cop. Marble was an ace detective with numerous awards and commendations, who eventually found himself on the wrong side of the law. He was working for the mob.

Marble and his partner carried out a few hits for the mob while being officers. Not only were they accused of those murders but they arrested individuals and surrendered them to the mob for them to be tortured and or be executed by members of the mob.

Eventually investigations led to Marble and his partner and they were both charged with four counts of first degree murder, Marble's partner committed suicide before he could be arrested, therefore Marble's lawyers threw all the blame on the dead cop. The government knew that it would be a dog fight to convict Marble since his lawyers were laying all the blame at his dead partner's feet. As a result Marble struck a deal with prosecutors and it earned him five years in the pen there is where he met Scar.

Now once again they would have to resort to their past training to get them out of this jam. They were a bit scared but trusted each other to come out safely. The two thugs had no intention of going down without a fight.

When they got into a desolate area, Marble suddenly accelerated and just as suddenly as he accelerated he stepped on the brakes within ten seconds throwing Jerome in a lurch forward. At the same time Scar leaned over and grabbed Jerome's gun, Jerome held on to the gun. In the scuffle for possession of the gun it went off. Marble was struck somewhere in the back. By this time the car had come to a halt and Jerome quickly opened the door and rolled out of the car. Jerome knew the area well and went down an embankment climbed a nearby fence made his way across the park and in no time signaled a cab and was out of the area and in the Diocese. Jerome still had the gun which he returned to the vestry.

In less than five minutes the police and EMS arrived on the scene and transported Marble to a nearby hospital. Marble had to undergo surgery to remove the bullet which was lodged in his back and had done damage to his spine. It was likely that Marble would be paralyzed from the waist down. Marble's recovery would be long and slow, however, when he regained consciousness Marble or Scar refused to tell investigators the name of the person or persons involved with the shooting. There was no eye witness. Police used tracker dogs but the dogs lost the scent at the point where Jerome hopped in the cab.

Scar told the cops that they were ambushed by a stranger; apparently the perpetrator was after the rental car they were driving. They explained that they were scared for their life and the only choice Marble had, was to do what he did to disarm the perpetrator.

The thugs described what happened in detail but avoided telling the cops that Fr. Jerome was the shooter. They pretended that they did not know the suspect. It would have been unusual if those thugs told the cops about Jerome; they would take care of Fr. Jerome by themselves. That is what they called street justice.

Jerome made it safely to the Diocese and was on the phone immediately to Foggy. At first the answering service picked up, it was Foggy's voice on the greeting, so Jerome knew he had dialed the correct phone number.

Even though Ray had dealt with Foggy, he did not know what Foggy had turned out to be after their days at school.

Jerome knew a lot more about foggy than his brother knew; now Jerome's thoughts were on Foggy.

He knew he needed another favor of his friend. The

female disguise Foggy had sent Jerome had worked like a dream but now Jerome knew he had to make a run for it because his female disguise could not be used in the Diocese if and when those two thugs came calling at the Diocese a second time. His father was not even aware of what had taken place in recent times.

Jerome knew it was inevitable they would return but this time unannounced. Jerome had no idea that Marble was shot even though he thought that there was a possibility. Jerome's thoughts were on Foggy. He dialed the number again the answering service once again picked up.

He would be happier if he could contact Ray but his brother's whereabouts were unknown. He knew Foggy would be able to shed some light on Ray's activities.

Jerome reflected on Foggy. He knew he had but a short time to leave the Diocese since he thought that at any moment the deadly tag team would arrive, once the heat from the investigation died down

Jerome was thankful he knew Foggy and kept in touch. But now Jerome would have to keep trying.

Foggy attempted to return Jerome's call but Jerome could not be located for some time by the Diocese staff.

Meanwhile the trial of Cindy and Rob was fast approaching the end and the defense still could not locate this mysterious witness who could shed light on this old lady that was seen leaving the scene of the crime without this witness the defense did not have much of a case Mr. Cottrell utilized two days cross examining the ballistics expert to extend the trial, to give the defense team an extra few days to find their mystery witness. Mr. Cottrell did a fantastic job. At one point the ballistic expert admitted that they did not find the gun that killed Jasmine and that there was no trace when the slug was traced by AFAAS that is the national data base system for all fired bullets. So without the gun or a trace of the owner the gun could be in any state and it did not necessarily mean that Rob or Cindy had possession of that gun on the night of the murder.

The investigation of the shooting of the two thugs were continuing the cops found Jerome's fingerprints but was unable to find a match simply because Jerome had a clean criminal record anyway the finger prints would remain on file for future reference. The bullet that was taken out of Marble's body was forwarded to AFAAS for comparison just in case the gun was used in the commission of another crime. It would take a few days for the results to come back.

Ray remained in Las Vegas living it up on the stolen money he was becoming a big loser night after night, but could not help himself. Ray sent his father a check for twenty thousand to take care of a financial debt he told his father he had, it would not raise suspicion because it was treated as a contribution to the church through Mary in the account of the Bartogs. Fr. Thom would be able to at least pay off some of Mr. Mentz's expenses associated with Cindy's trial.

Eventually Cindy decided to tell Mr. Mentz all that went on with Jerome/Hector and gradually it dawned on Mr. Mentz that there was more to the shooting of Jasmine than he now realized. His first thought was that Cindy was the intended victim and that Jasmine was in the wrong place at the wrong time. Now the theory of the tall old lady made sense to him the tall old lady could be a disguised male because it was rare to find a tall old lady taller than six feet most tall women tend to lose height in their latter days due to osteoporosis.

Mr. Mentz would be faced with an ethical dilemma, how he could send his investigators to question the son of his client that was paying his bill? Nevertheless Cindy's father wants the truth which will vindicate his daughter. If in fact Jerome did the crime he had no choice but to do the time.

Mr. Mentz spent several restless nights as the trial neared the end his focus was whether he could put Cindy on the stand to use some of the information she had given and secondly he was verbally preparing his summation. Mr. Mentz knew in the absence of a strong outstanding defense he needed an outstanding closing statement. He also knew that even if he should put Cindy on the stand he would be throwing light on a situation his childhood friend preferred not to have exposed.

Mr. Mentz finally decided it would be better for his case if Cindy did not take the stand.

Jimmy remained in custody as a conspirator in the armored car heist. Six months later and two bond hearing, the Feds were happy to keep him in custody.

Even though they could not link him to the robbery of the armored car his legal team presented to the judge at all the hearings that Jimmy was only the driver of the armored car and he was being victimized because the Feds could not recover more than seventy five percent of the loot Jimmy's lawyers went on to say that whoever planned the heist planned it properly or carefully and because it was well executed and they had no answer then they surmised that Jimmy was part of the plot, the lawyers also stated that their client was knocked to the ground in a semi conscious condition and he did not even see what hit him.

The premise of the charge to hold Jimmy was that the Feds thought he would be a flight risk and on the other hand once he is charged he could be held indefinitely pending investigation which was ongoing. The judge was willing to let Jimmy out on bond but the identity theft had done him in.

The Feds decided to go ahead with the identity theft charges hoping Jimmy would be sentenced to a year in jail to give them enough time to complete the armored car investigation.

The two disciples remained defiant; the Feds continued to quiz the two robbers daily. They were offered several deals, but to no avail they would not crack despite the daily quizzing. Paul looked vulnerable and the Feds were concentrating their efforts on Paul they wanted him to finger Jimmy as part of the plot to rob the armored car and they also wanted to know who was James. If they could get a surname they would be on the right track to apprehend the mastermind all that was recovered was less than a quarter of the money. The recovery of the money was the Feds main focus. Yet to get the money they had to apprehend the mastermind of the robbery James.

They got that name from an anonymous tip. The tipster was Martha, the motel maid. Martha did not know what she was doing but she was hoping everyone that participated in the heist would get caught so she could go free with the ten thousand, which by this time had already been exhausted.

Jerome finally got in touch with Mitch (nicknamed) Foggy and departed for Ohio the following day after the shooting. Jerome was cautious as he left the Diocese at four am for the greyhound terminal, by this time he was aware that Marble was in critical but stable condition. Jerome was hoping that Marble pull through his injury. The last thing Jerome wanted was another murder on his hands. Jerome's trip to Ohio was uneventful because as yet the investigation did not lead to him. He was met by Foggy at the greyhound bus stand on arrival. Jerome was delighted to reunite with his buddy Foggy.

They stayed up all night talking about old times. Eventually Jerome divulged all the trouble he was in including Jasmine murder the trial of Cindy and his doubts if Cindy knew he was Hector or not. When Jerome was done he felt a great relief, to him it seemed better than any confession he had ever taken.

Jerome once again could not even try to piece together the sudden twists and turns his life had suddenly taken. First it was Cindy's allegation of rape then thanks to her mother and Fr. Thom they resolved a settlement. Then just when Jerome thought it was over along came Cindy again for more money.

Foggy confirmed that Ray passed through with a woman named Mary. Foggy showed what his brother now looked like and told Jerome that his brother was back in Vegas living it up. Ray was convinced that his brother had carried out the armored car heist and had a lot of cash on hand; Jerome could not understand why he took Mary along with him.

Jerome now reflected on what was said, the truth you rob a bank and you may get away free, you kill and the cops will hunt you to the bitter end. There is no statute of limitations where murder is concerned. Jerome was hoping he could go back in time and undo Jasmine's murder because if Marble died he would not only be looking at one murder but two. He shuddered at the thought of a priest being convicted of one murder and now two. Jerome knew he would be looking at the death penalty or life in prison.

Rob and Cindy's fate was now in the hands of the jury after lengthy summations by all the attorneys involved it took the jury four days of deliberation. On the fourth day the jury sent the judge a note that they were hopelessly deadlocked, the judge called the jury in and instructed them to try a little harder. After another two full days the jury was still deadlocked so the judge declared a mistrial. Cindy and Rob would have to undergo another trial and endure being in custody until a new trial date could be announced. Mentz declared a victory for the defense. Because now he had new information that could shed light on whom the real killer was. Mr. Mentz knew now that he had time to carry out a full investigation and he knew in which direction to start with this investigation.

Mr. Mentz arranged to meet with Fr. Thom and Jerome on his way back to New York now that the media frenzy was over the trial was done and now no one would be following him.

Olga was high in her praise for the way in which Mr. Mentz handled this trial. She knew that he had done the best that he could do under the circumstances Olga did not know the significance behind the tall old lady. Mr. Mentz instructed Cindy not to disclose what she knew to any one, not even her mother because he wanted to surprise his main suspect with the secrecy element.

Mr. Mentz assured Cindy that had she divulged this information earlier he would have been able to bring the person he thought killed Jasmine to justice and that he was now more convinced that Cindy and Rob were innocent. Cindy remained in custody awaiting her new trial while Mr. Mentz would put his full investigation team on Jerome.

Jerome was a step ahead of Mr. Mentz and his investigation team and Fr. Thom could not tell Jerome's whereabouts.

One day after the mistrial verdict Mr. Mentz paid the Diocese a visit, he was Fr. Thom's hero he brought his childhood friend up to date with what went on during the trial he made mention of Cindy and her mother's reunion and informed Thom that her mother was present every day of the trial including the first of the three days the trial was suspended. His visit was now not a social call or was is to collect a debt. Nevertheless he told his friend that his expenses were fifteen thousand dollars and he really was not looking to collect at that time however, Fr. Thom was more than happy to pay him in cash from the money Ray had sent him.

Mr. Mentz had other important questions to ask the old priest, but because of their close relationship over the years found it difficult to begin. He was just about to ask for Jerome when the phone rang, it was Jerome on the line. Jerome took care to call his father from a pay phone. Jerome knew that even though the Diocese did not have caller ID his call could be traced from phone records and he was not about to give away his position because he did not know how long he would be in hiding. Jerome intention would be to play things by ear until he knew it was safe to return he was even thinking to join his brother on the run and never return to the Diocese for fear for his life as well as the law.

Just imagine how shocked he was when after speaking briefly to his father and explaining that something had happened, that he would be away for a couple days. Jerome went on to let his father know he was safe but just wanted him to know he had to do what he did for his safety.

Mr. Mentz came on the phone after exchanging pleasantries he went to work right away. He started to question Jerome about his whereabouts on the night of Jasmine's murder. Jerome said that the date did not ring a bell and it was more than a year ago. Mr. Mentz was about to ask Jerome another question but Jerome was more than happy to hear the computer voice say he only had one minute. Jerome stalled for time claiming he could not hear Mr. Mentz and purposely let the time run out.

Mr. Mentz now turned to Fr. Thom and asked him if Jerome made it a point to leave without the permission of the church since he was in their employ so to speak.

Fr. Thom told the lawyer that the past eighteen months has been really rocky with his son, his whole attitude and demeanor has changed since Cindy started calling the Diocese.

Fr. Thom was more than happy to talk about the situation, he had no one to turn to with his problems associated with Cindy's calls except Jerome and he explained he always tried to speak to her rather than let Jerome have dialogue with her.

Fr. Thom reassured Mr. Mentz that he would be able to say if Jerome was at the Diocese on the day of Jasmine's murder. Mentz told Fr. Thom that it was of vital importance that he not confront his son with that information even if he was away. He should let his investigators question Jerome if need be.

Fr. Thom paid Mr. Mentz in cash and thanked him then told him to hang on for a second while he checked if Jerome was at the Diocese on September 11th 2006.

It did not take Fr. Thom more than five minutes to return with the information. Jerome had disappeared like he did this time on the ninth of September and

The Deadly Priest

returned on the twelfth of September. Mr. Mentz was ecstatic he knew he had the answer he was looking for but how could he break the news to his friend that this son might be the disguised tall lady. Mr. Mentz did not even want to tell his friend that Jerome might very well be responsible for the death of Jasmine.

Mr. Mentz asked Fr. Thom one more question - did Jerome know that I was coming here to see you? Fr. Thom's reply was yes. Mentz figured that Jerome excused himself to avoid his questions but did not tell Fr. Thom what he thought. Mr. Mentz finally excused himself by telling Fr. Thom he had a plane to catch and left after a few drinks.

Fr. Thom was puzzled at the type of questions his friend asked about Jerome. But then Jerome had no motive or reason to kill Jasmine. Why would he want to kill Cindy's friend. This did not add up, it makes no sense.

This is the reason I tried to keep Jerome from speaking to Cindy Fr. Thom reasoned to himself.

Fr. Thom stayed up until the wee hours of the new day trying to put the pieces together, he could not bring himself to believe Jerome had something to do with Cindy in Albany let alone kill Jasmine the situation was not making any sense to him. Fr. Thom said he would have to contact his friend tomorrow to find out what he was driving at.

In the meantime, Fr. Jerome felt sick to his stomach he always knew Mr. Mentz was a brilliant attorney and based on his questions it was apparent that

Cindy had told him something or everything. Jerome felt like his world was caving in on him. He was dazed and when he returned to Foggy's home, he went to bed immediately

Jerome needed time to plan his next move. He needed to speak to Foggy but still at the same time did not feel like speaking. He just needed quiet time to himself.

The following day Fr. Thom tried in vain to contact Mr. Mentz, he was told Mr. Mentz was in court and would not be returning to his office for the remainder of the day.

Mr. Mentz's habit was to take a few days off after he completed a case. He was only appearing in court briefly to request another date for a pending trial then he would fly out to the Bahamas for a few days of relaxation.

The following day, two detectives paid Fr .Thom a visit. AFAAS had matched the bullet to the type of gun registered to Fr. Thom. A Smith and Wesson, thirty eight caliber.

What the detectives did not tell Fr. Thom was that the bullets that killed Jasmine and the bullet that shot Marble were a perfect match and since the incident with Marble happened so close to the church they had their suspicion.

They needed his gun for comparison. Fr. Thom could not locate the gun where it was usually kept. He told the detectives that Jerome was the one that used the gun from time to time on the shooting range. That he has not seen the gun in awhile, not that he ever checked for it. The detectives asked to speak to Jerome and Fr. Thom told the detectives he was away on business from the information Fr. Thom provided the detectives his son left the day following the shooting.

The detectives left without asking any more questions but they secured a search warrant and returned to the Diocese in search of the gun. It did not take them long to find the gun in a closet in Jerome's room. Jerome was not taking chances he kept the gun close by since he became aware that Marble and Scar were in town. In his haste to leave he did not return the gun to the locked case in which his father kept the gun.

The gun was sent to the crime lab, test fired and found to be the murder weapon that killed Jas and also the same weapon that shot Marble.

Jerome was nowhere to be found. Fr. Thom was taken to police headquarters to answer questions about the gun and his son. Fr. Thom explained that Jerome was the person who used the gun at the shooting range. He said he did not have possession or handle the gun in more than ten years. When questioned about Jerome, he said Jerome left without disclosing his whereabouts. Fr. Thom said that since he left he had called only once and did not say where he was. The detectives asked Fr. Thom if he would be willing to take a lie detector test and he consented. The cops were convinced that Fr. Thom was telling the truth so they did not administer the lie detector test. They only asked the question to see his reaction.

The Deadly Priest

After three weeks of searching for Jerome he was featured on America Most Wanted. Just imagine the media coverage this new development was attracting. Media vehicles were camped outside the Diocese. The media was trying to interview church members about the type of priest Fr. Jerome was and his schedule regularity at the Diocese. They were focusing on the dates of the Massachusetts murder. Did he have an alibi? Fr. Thom refused to answer questions from the media.

Ray always looked at America Most Wanted every Saturday it was aired because it was his way of knowing what was going on if the Feds were on to him.

He was shocked to see his twin brother on AMW as a murder suspect. Ray immediately contacted Foggy to find out what was going. Foggy said that Jerome was hiding out at a friend of his; Ray was more than happy that he had changed his identity so he no longer looked identical to Jerome. But Ray was taking no chances he would stay out of sight as much as possible.

The police obtained a warrant for the phone records of the Diocese they found only one call from out of town and it matched the date Fr. Thom said his son called.

The police in Massachusetts contacted their counterparts in Ohio but it turned out that the call was made from a pay phone. There were more than thirty calls made to Foggy's phone number, from the Diocese. Therefore they were focusing their attention on Ohio.

The police in Ohio made a sudden sweep at Foggy friend's home where Jerome was hiding out, after several days of surveillance and good police work. The cops questioned a convicted felon who was on parole and working the streets, which is a violation of her probation the police got lucky because she was hired by Foggy to entertain Jerome, at his hiding place. Unfortunately, Jerome's hiding place was under surveillance when the prostitute visited him.

She was well known by law enforcement. Shaquita Powers was arrested several times for prostitution. As she departed from Jerome's hide out the following day, she was arrested and questioned about Jerome. With an obvious threat to be returned to prison for parole violation if she did not cooperate, because she was high on some type of substance when arrested, Shaquita immediately complied with the detectives and confirmed that Jerome was alone in the house. Shaquita was tired of being in and out of prison so she gave Jerome up for her freedom. She did not have a choice but to speak the truth. She knew how the cops worked and eventually when the cops found out she was lying for a John she barely knew, it would make things bad for her. Shaquita was trying her utmost best to stay out of prison, at least for a while. She knew that SWAT would eventually storm the house and find him.

Jerome could no longer leave that house without being arrested and it was only a matter of time before the dragnet would close in on him. Once he was profiled on AMW it seemed to go all downhill for Jerome. He knew his time had come and now his only hope of freedom was to remain indoors as much as possible and this is why the prostitute was sent to the house for his entertainment.

Jerome remembered his brother's words "you rob a bank you may get away but murder they will hunt you down to the bitter end."

In less than one hour after the prostitute left his secret hiding place, Jerome was arrested by SWAT without incident. He was immediately questioned by Detective Hill and Captain Johnson from the Ohio North Detective Squad. He confessed to the shooting of Marble claiming it was in self defense. But when the questioning turned to Jasmine, Jerome told the detectives he would like to speak to his lawyer. Jerome waived his right to be extradited to Massachusetts so he was transported without incident.

Now the media was having a field day. The headlines read in bold.

===

THE DEADLY PRIEST

===

Marble recovered from his gunshot wound and was now listed stable out of danger. His progress was slow at first, but eventually he was transferred to a rehab unit where he would undergo months of therapy. Marble pushed himself to recover; his main focus was revenge. Revenge was making him work harder. He was making tremendous progress. Marble did everything he was told to do and even more. His progress was ahead of schedule and within six months Marble was walking with the assistance of a walker his doctor and physical therapist were simply amazed at his progress.

Two months later Marble could walk on his own without assistance. His therapist advised that he increase the distance he walked on a weekly basis. Marble increased his distance on a daily basis rather than weekly.

Now with Jerome no longer on the run, no one was looking for Ray. The thing about Ray was that no one knew his involvement with the heist, except Jimmy and the two disciples John and Paul. Ray was having fun living it up at the casinos in Vegas.

Fr. Thom finally got in touch with Mr. Mentz. He told him that Jerome was linked to the murder of Jasmine through ballistics. Mr. Mentz also told Fr. Thom about Hector the investigator. He told Fr. Thom he was only made aware of these circumstances at the end of the trial by Cindy. He said that she was afraid to reveal this information because she thought that she could be further charged with extortion. Mr. Mentz apologized to Fr. Thom, stating that he was happy that his client Cindy would now be vindicated, but he was sorry it had to be this way - that she would be vindicated at the expense of his son and insisted that if Fr. Jerome did the crime, he would naturally have to do the time.

Mentz also informed Fr. Thom that he would petition the court to have all charges against Cindy dropped in the light of these new developments. He told Fr. Thom that he was not going to be able to represent Jerome in Albany due to a conflict of interest. He could possibly be available for his case in Massachusetts if Fr. Thom needed his services and if he was charged with the attempted murder of Marble.

And in fact, Fr. Jerome was arraigned on charges of attempted murder of Marble just like Mr. Mentz had told his father. Mentz sent a lawyer in his place just for the arraignment. He did not want to appear for Jerome who would be eventually charged for the murder of Jasmine. If he did appear at the arraignment, it would raise serious questions as to if he knew that Jerome was in fact the tall old lady that was seen leaving the scene of the crime after Jasmine's murder.

Fr .Thom was flabbergasted when he got off the phone with Mr. Mentz, his boyhood friend. He was upset and angry. Fr. Thom questioned himself, had he done things differently would the outcome would be different? He thought about Ray. Despite his wayward ways Ray never brought him shame and disgrace like Jerome had done.

Should he have let Jerome lead his own life, would this have happened? He tried to keep Jerome in the church so he would have good morals and ethics. Now look at what a mess he had made for himself and the church. The story of Jerome was all over the news. News vans swarmed the church looking for a news story. Even Olga was on the news these days, she appeared on several talk shows saying that she was happy her daughter was vindicated and all along she knew her daughter was innocent.

Mr. Mentz and Mr. Cottrell submitted a motion to the judge on Cindy's case. In the judge's chambers along with the prosecutor, Mr. Nelson and his assistant asked for all charges to be dropped in the light of new evidence. The defense team described the ballistics reports that linked the murder weapon to Jerome and stated all along that the defense team had heard of a witness who could still not be located that saw a tall old lady leaving the scene of the shooting.

Mr. Mentz went on, "In all likelihood the tall old lady would be Jerome in disguise because no other person or persons except Jerome and his father had access to the gun which now is a perfect match to the murder weapon."

The prosecution agreed with the defense submission and has agreed to dismiss all charges against Cindy and Robert for the murder of Jasmine.

Cindy and Rob would be released in a couple of days once all the paperwork was completed. Olga thanked Mr. Mentz greatly and informed him that she was planning a great home coming welcome for Cindy. Sponsored by members of the media for publicity and as a public apology for all the things they had written about the two defendants. In less than a week Cindy would be a free member of society again.

Jerome would now have to face trial for the death of Jasmine O'Hare as well as the shooting of Marble.

In the meanwhile the mastermind behind the heist still remained a mystery. Jimmy remained in custody and Paul and John sentencing date was quickly approaching. They would soon be sentenced and began to serve time for their participation in the heist. The two disciples as they were now known still continued to remain defiant. The authorities wanted them to finger Jimmy as an accomplice which they were not prepared to do despite the circumstances.

It would be Thanksgiving in exactly one week from the date slated for Cindy's release; Cindy was now sitting in prison for almost eighteen months. She had spent her last Christmas behind bars and was now looking forward to her freedom by year's end when she was hit with a verdict of a mistrial. She knew she would have to spend another year in prison other inmates had told Cindy that her new trial would come up a lot faster than the time she had to wait for her first trial but that was little consolation to Cindy since she wanted to be out before Christmas so imagine how elated she was when she received the news that she would soon be released from her attorney.

This was going to be the best Thanksgiving she would have and there would be a lot to give thanks for. First of all, Cindy was thankful to God, then to her attorney as well as Fr. Thom and her mother who persuaded Fr. Thom that he had no other alternative than to provide Cindy with a lawyer. Cindy was more than happy that for the very first time as far back as she could remember she had her sober mother. It was a great relief to be reunited with her mother whom she did not see or hear from in more than five years, and now that she was clean, was a plus.

Cindy was reflecting on what her first day of freedom would be like when she was told that she had a visitor. To her surprise it was her mother accompanied by Fr. Thom.

Fr. Thom still did not disclose to anyone that he might be Cindy's father, but visited her under the guise that he wanted to publicly apologize to her for her wrongful arrest and detention for the death of her friend. When questioned by the media if his son had committed this murder, Fr. Thom's reply was let us not prejudge my son like we did with Cindy and Rob; a man is innocent until proven guilty and that he will stand by his son even in these difficult circumstances. He went on to say that it is difficult to comprehend if and when this murder took place and he would like to listen to the prosecution's case.

In an exclusive interview, he said that his son said that he was innocent of the murder of Jasmine but he did admit to shooting Marble in self defense after he was kidnapped and he presumed his life was in danger. Fr. Thom added that there were still a lot of questions about this whole situation that needed to be explained and he did not have enough time as yet to sit down with his son to find out all the details. He told them emphatically that he would not discuss the merit of the case any further until after he speaks to his son and his attorney. Fr. Thom brought the impromptu press conference to a close. Amidst shouts to Olga what plans have you got for your daughter when she is released? Olga ignored the question as they were admitted to the jail for their visit with Cindy.

Amidst legal wrangling as to where Jerome should be tried, first the Governors of Massachusetts and New York stepped in to work out an agreement that Jerome would be transferred for his second trial as soon as the first trial was over. The governors agreed to let the judicial system decide which trial would be first and in all likelihood the murder of Jasmine should take priority. Eventually, it was decided that Fr. Jerome would be tried first for the death of Jasmine O'Hare in December, in Albany. His defense team was already at work filing motions to have the trial start in February of the next year to give the defense team time to prepare their case. This time, Fr .Thom did not have to worry about paying for his son's defense; the church had an obligation to pay for any priest that was in trouble as a means of protecting the church's good name.

The Deadly Priest

Jerome's attorneys hammered out a deal with both DA's, that in exchange for a guilty plea to both crimes, the prosecution in Albany would not seek the death penalty. The guilty plea also meant that Fr Jerome will not be further humiliated with the media circus at a trial. There was hardly any protest from the parents of Jasmin or Rob. Seems everyone was happy with the outcome.

Fr. Jerome was sentenced to life without parole and remains in a correctional institution. Ray never visited his brother.

Jimmy was released due to insufficient evidence of his participation in the heist but the investigation was never closed. Paul and John, the two disciples as they were called, were both sentenced to fifteen years.

Ray remained on the lamb posing as Henry Bertog. He was never charged with the heist and the thugs were nowhere near locating him due to his new identity. Six months after Cindy's release her mother relapsed and went back to jail. Fr. Thom and Cindy quietly went and did the DNA test to satisfy their curiosity. They were both disappointed to find out that Fr. Thom was not Cindy's father. They agreed to keep in touch. In less than a year Cindy got married and moved back to Massachusetts to be close to Fr. Thom.

Fr. Thom died a year after Cindy's move. Two years later, Cindy gave birth to a healthy boy. She continues to dread Fall and Winter but now, with her new husband Ken, it doesn't seem so bad.

The Deadly Priest